The Holiday Delay

Cassandra Moll

Other Titles By Cassandra Moll

The Golden City Series
The Boards Between Us
The Shots Against Us
The Last Drive Home

The Maple Grove Series
Beautifully Broken
Daring Destiny

Author's Note

D ear Reader,

What's goin' on!? Burnsey here—

I just wanted to let you in on a little secret—this isn't my debut! Although you can totally read *The Holiday Delay* on its own—and should if it's around the holidays, duh!—you first meet me and some of the other characters discussed in this story in other books.

If you've already read those—*The Boards Between Us* and *The Shots Against Us* (the first two books in the Golden City Series)—then you're all set! You know everything you need to know to get the most from this novella. If you haven't and you're still ready to start here with *our* story, who could blame ya? The *Burns' Effect* is strong, eh?

Regardless of where you're starting, you won't be disappointed. I mean, it's me! What else could you need, am I right?

Now, go! Get reading! Some of us have a plane to catch...

See ya on the other side!

Brett

THE HOLIDAY DELAY

Cassandra Moll

1
Nellie

"You have got to be kidding me."

I look out the window to nothing but white powder and stopped cars—horns honking sporadically around me the same way Pop Rocks bounce across your tongue. The wind pulls snow in each direction like disorganized brushstrokes slapped onto a canvas.

"The roads are all sorts of jacked up. No one's moving," my Uber driver calls over his shoulder, laying on his horn and only adding to the noise. "And this isn't even the drop-off lane."

I sigh, looking down at my sketchbook, then glance at my watch. Leaning closer to my window, I squint in an attempt to see through the flurries. "How much further?"

At this rate my increased heartbeat matches the pulse of the horns coming from every car thinking *their* honk might be the one that gets things moving. My flight is set to board in twenty minutes, and I still have to make it through security.

"Uhh..." Sunny—or at least that's what the app says his name is—leans over the steering wheel for a better look. "I want to say just another minute, but I'm literally in park, so..."

I blow a heavy breath through my lips, cursing the irony of Sunny's name—and his perfect cheekbones—along with the poorly timed nor' easter hitting Golden City. It's as if G.C. is warning me not to leave—attempting to save me from the impending torture that is returning to my one-stoplight town.

If only I could listen.

With a deep inhale, I reach between my feet and drop my sketchbook with the cover still flipped open into the back pocket of my grey neoprene backpack. Shocker—once again, it seems to be a bad omen. I lean across the back seat, slipping my hand under the various strands of roped string and satin ribbon that serve as the handles of my gift bags. "I'll just walk from here," I say, pulling them into my lap.

"You sure?" Sunny asks, his gaze meeting mine in the rearview mirror.

Not even a little bit.

"Definitely," I answer, glancing down at my watch—eighteen minutes.

He turns his lips in and furrows his brow as if he's considering whether to let me leave. I latch on to the thought that he's a decent guy who doesn't want me to get swept up by the blizzard and push away the idea that he might have planned to kidnap me and use my skin as wallpaper.

Sunny smiles in a way that *could* be genuine—or could be murderous. "Alright, let me get your suitcase for you."

"Oh, no, that's okay. It's small." I pull the hood of my black, padded winter coat up over my head. "Besides, it's coming down sideways, and I already have to get out. If you could just pop it open, I'll grab it and slip under the overhang. But thank you."

Sunny nods slowly and pops the trunk with the click of a button.

He thinks I'm being nice. In reality, the idea of my 5' 8" body standing in front of an open trunk with snow criss-crossing so ferociously that it makes any visibility nearly impossible... scares me shitless. Maybe my sketchbook's good for something after all—now I have evidence in my backpack in the form of his shaded profile.

Damn, I have got to stop listening to true crime podcasts.

"Be careful out there," he calls as I open the door.

Yeah... that could be sweet—or it could be a subliminal warning.

"Thanks! You too!"

After grabbing my bag from the floor by my feet, I step out of the car and throw the door closed. Rounding the back, I bend forward to counteract the force of the wind. Considering my destination and the weather I'm enduring for it, I suddenly start questioning whether Sunny's skinning or shoving me into the trunk of a red Honda would really be as bad as it sounds.

I swing my straps over my shoulders and let the gift bags slide into the crook of my elbow before finally reaching my pale pink, hardshell carry-on. I yank it from Sunny's trunk, but not before noticing it's empty except for my luggage.

Empty and clean.

Maybe too clean.

Slamming it shut, I race for the sidewalk under the overhang, hoping to shield myself from the whipping winds and put distance between me and my possible—yet very improbable—attacker. Looking up, I spot my airline only a few doors away, and I book it through the entrance.

I head right for security, grateful not to have a bag to check. I think I packed light, hoping the idea of less stuff would strengthen the illusion that the time would pass quickly. But right now, with approximately thirteen minutes to get through security and to my gate, the reason for my lack of luggage is irrelevant.

Moving for the stairs, I bob and weave around pedestrians with much more time on their hands than I have, apparently. I take the steps two at a time, nearly growling as I carry my small suitcase by the handle, the weight pulling at my shoulder as the hard plastic bounces off of my calf.

The only thing going through my mind besides the fact that I can not miss this flight and screw Liam over is that the possibility of this exact circumstance is reason number... *whatever*... that I never go home.

Especially at Christmas.

"Delayed? This has to be a joke." My arms go slack, and my bags slide from my wrist to the floor as I groan under my breath. "I knew I should have stayed home," I continue mumbling. "I could be two hot toddies and three episodes of Love Island deep by now."

As if to mock me, my phone vibrates in my pocket and brings me back to reality. I glance over both shoulders, hoping no one at either over-crowded gate to my left or right overheard me talking to myself.

"*And* I wouldn't look like a total lunatic in public," I add in a low whisper, unintentionally choosing to continue the conversation.

I pull out my cell, accidentally bumping the handle of my small suitcase standing tall beside me. The hit causes the carry-on to teeter back and forth before conveniently falling directly onto the three gift bags now squished beneath it. *Fantastic.*

I groan, partly because of the mess beside me and partly because of the text from my mother reminding me I'll be in my hometown in just a matter of hours. Choosing to deal with the annoyance at the gate rather than in my life, I spin around, leaning toward the floor.

At the same time, a voice floats toward me.

"Oh, here let me—"

Before I can stop myself, I slam into its owner, my forehead colliding with something rock hard.

"Shit, wat—"

"Oh, my ba—"

We speak simultaneously, him stumbling over his apology and me realizing the surface I smacked into isn't a wall—it's a thigh. When I throw my head up, I manage to knock it once again on yet another appendage that's just as solid.

This time, a massive hand.

"Oh my God."

A massive hand wrapped around a steaming cup of coffee.

"Woah."

My gaze snaps up—and up—until I finally spot the face of the man I nearly assaulted... and mutilated with a latte. A face I recognize.

"Oh... I'm... uh... " I try to maintain my previous grouchiness, all things considered, but I'm left too flustered to give it any real umph. "So sorry," I finish softly.

Brett Burns, defenseman and resident goofball of the Golden City Flames, scans his now damp tan peacoat and chuckles. "Don't be. Stuff like this actually happens to me all the time. It's fine."

I shake my head, already unwrapping my scarf in a desperate attempt to fix the mess and undo my reaction. I shove down what's left of my annoyance about this trip and press the ball of fabric to his wet jacket. "No, it's definitely not."

Nothing about today is fine.

I'm still rambling when I realize my hand has drifted from his noticeably wall-like chest toward his crotch. Heat floods my face as I yank my hand away, balling the scarf up awkwardly in my hands. "Shit. Sorry. Again."

Brett, who hasn't technically told me his name, presses his fingertips to the wool as he attempts to hide a grin. "Wow, that's actually so hot."

Everywhere north of my collarbone blazes, and he definitely notices.

"The coffee," he clarifies, glancing down at the stain then back up at me. "I meant the, uh... " He clears his throat through his smirk. "The coffee."

I shake my head uncontrollably in the hopes that, like an Etch A Sketch, it will somehow erase the last two minutes. "Right, yeah, no. I know."

Brett switches his dripping cup to his other hand and wipes his palm on his already wet coat. At the same time, I lean down and gather my now concave gift bags.

"Brett, by the way," he says, extending his hand toward me.

I wiggle the bags into the crook of my arm, reaching to meet it too quickly, my adrenaline not yet depleted from the rush of the last half hour. "Oh, I... "

I stop myself before finishing the thought that almost escapes naturally.

"I'm Nellie," I pivot.

Brett narrows his eyes.

Apparently, my face didn't get the memo.

"Did you know that already?" he asks, leaning in. "My name?"

My lips curl as I tuck a strand of my undoubtedly frizzy strawberry hair behind my ear. "I did," I admit.

He nods knowingly, slurping—almost attractively?—from the coffee pooled along the rim of his lid. "Flames fan?"

I tilt my head back and forth. "I guess, technically," I say. His brow furrows. "But I'm also a Montgomery employee, so... mostly that."

"What? No way. Monte?"

I shrug. "I guess, technically," I repeat in the same coy tone. Brett stares at me blankly, waiting for more. "I'm Liam's nanny," I clarify. "Well, not *his* nanny. His daughter's."

Damn, Nell. Stop talking.

"Oh, no shit."

He smiles wide, and the typical image of Brett "Burnsey" Burns flashes before my eyes. It's even more endearing off-screen—all bright white teeth and charming baby blues. I always wondered if it was all a show, but it seems his Golden Retriever vibes might be natural after all.

"Ruthie's dad, right?" he asks, bringing me back to the moment.

"Yeah," I say, grinning for the first time. "She's the best."

He nods in agreement, his mouth still set in that ear-to-ear smile.

A silence falls between us—the first moment of calm I've had since Sunny may or may not have been plotting my kidnapping. If I had any emotional energy left, I might be more on edge.

Do I flirt with him?

Will he ask for my number?

Is talking to him weird since he and my boss seem to run in the same circle?

But between the afternoon I've had and what's waiting for me on the other side of this delay, I have no more nerves or anxious energy to spend. And very little good mood to spare.

"Is your flight delayed too?" I ask simply, genuinely curious.

Brett tips his chin down, glancing around the crowded room. I mimic him, really searching the holding area for the first time since this whole debacle started. Many people are in their own little worlds—curled up in sweatshirts with headphones in and hoods pulled low or nose-deep in their phones and Kindles. But those who aren't hiding behind technology or sitting at the bar in the center of the room deep in conversation fueled by Jack and Cokes and Christmas spirit, are staring.

At us.

"Yeah, I think they all are," Brett says, but his voice hits me weakly, muffled by the unwanted attention.

"What?" I ask, slowly making indirect eye contact with a girl around my age with an open mouth and high brows. I follow her gaze that's just slightly off mine to the broad defenseman hovering over me with floppy chestnut hair and a caramel-stained coat.

"The flights," he explains, scratching the back of his head. "Looks like we're grounded until morning."

Now he's got my attention.

"Oh, thank God," I blurt out.

The sigh that escapes me is entirely too dramatic, but I can't help it. This is the best news I've heard all day. Finally able to take a deep breath, I fill my lungs with air again and ignore the dozens of eyes still on me—or rather, Brett.

Who knew that seeing an athlete in Golden City was so rare? I guess, for me, it's just another weekday.

Brett chuckles, either reading my mind or responding to my relief. "That's a good thing?"

"Oh, well." I attempt to backtrack. What kind of person is happy to be stuck in an airport two days before Christmas? But again, my emotional exhaustion wins out.

At least my mood seems to have lifted. *How come I don't assume he's a predator too?*

"Yes, honestly, it is."

He takes a sip of his coffee, inhaling deeply as he does. I can't help but watch the way his throat moves up and down as he swallows. In my defense, it's completely opened up to me at this angle.

Damn, this man's tall.

"I sort of agree, actually."

My eyes go wide. I would have thought Brett was the antler-wearing, carol-singing, eggnog-chugging, Buddy the Elf type. But agreeing with me on holiday misery? "I guess there's something to unpack there for both of us then," I say, smiling and only half-kidding.

Brett runs his tongue over his teeth, his consistent smile dimming slightly before bouncing right back. "Well, do you plan to wait it out?"

I turn around toward the flight board again. It's still lit up like a Christmas tree with red-lettered cancellations blinking like twinkle lights.

For one delicious moment, I consider this a bow-wrapped gift—permission to go home, binge reality TV, and avoid another hometown holiday, no guilt necessary because... I tried! But then I remember the road conditions and near nonexistent possibility that any Ubers are even running right now.

"Considering the standstill traffic just twenty minutes ago, I'm pretty sure if I left I'd get back home just in time to turn around again."

Brett blows a breath through his lips. "Yeah, that's what I'm thinking." We both nod, glancing around again. "It could be fun to kill time here, though," he adds unexpectedly, his face bright. "Like a little adventure."

My brows arch as a smile plasters itself across my face.

There it is—that retriever mode we know and love.

"Yeah," I laugh, my previous grouch all but gone. "Maybe."

He hikes his backpack I'm just now noticing, up on his shoulders and shrugs. "Well, what do you say?" he asks, bringing his cup back to his lips. "I'll show you mine if you show me yours."

My lips part. If those words came from any other man, I think I'd throat punch him on instinct—ill intentions and all. But from what I've seen at games and in interviews, I'm not sure Brett could be offensive on purpose if he tried.

"I meant the, uh, baggage you talked about," he adds, dropping his coffee away from his mouth. "You know, the things we had to... " His voice fades as his arm slowly lowers to his side. "Unpack."

I blink a few times, cruelly soaking up his slight panic just a little.

He holds my stare for another beat before his face and shoulders drop. "I'm not a creep, I swear."

"Sure, that's what they all say," I mutter, Sunny's face unnecessarily coming to the forefront of my mind.

Brett winces and takes a sudden interest in his brown leather sneakers.

"But yeah," I add quickly, deciding being *alone* in a crowded airport where Christmas songs begin to drift slowly from the speakers might be worse than my intended destination. "What the hell? I'm in."

His face seems to glow as he somehow manages to stand even taller. "Cool," he says simply.

"Cool," I repeat.

And it is.

Because anything beats going home.

2

Brett

*D*amn.

I don't think I ever realized how many people truly fly this close to Christmas. This happens every year because of our schedule—sometimes with even less wiggle room before the holiday. But this is the first time I haven't had my mind set on walking into Mom's house to the smell of butter tarts in the oven and the sound of Dad yelling at the game on TV as always.

Of course it's busy—the city always is. But I guess I never realized how next-level nuts it truly gets thanks to the distraction I had in FaceTiming my sister to count down the hours. My focus is usually on just finally getting home.

But not this year.

Did I realize how many people would recognize me? I've been told I look different with my tongue in my mouth or when I'm not flipping on skates. Standing in the long line for my coffee as eyes slowly trailed over to me, I banked on that being true. But the second I walked toward the center of the madness, I felt them multiply.

My smile is well known. That could be part of the reason so many people have noticed I'm here, but I didn't realize how much I'd be showing it off with everything on my mind right now.

Maybe that's because I wasn't.

At least not until she came along.

Nellie.

I may or may not have seen her approach the board and start talking to herself. Like a magnet, I immediately decided I had to double check that my flight was, in fact, still delayed despite the announcement made at my gate only seconds before. I didn't imagine her spilling my coffee down my peacoat and testing the thickness of my cashmere sweater underneath, though. This jacket is new—fly as hell—and the perfect match to my shoes.

But that dry cleaning bill might be the best money ever spent.

"Alright, so do you want the broken chair here, the spot on the wall over there, or... " I lean forward, tilting my head past the luggage cart that's attempting to weave around pedestrians. "I think there might be some carpet space next to the trashcan, but full disclosure... the neighbors look suspicious."

Nellie follows my gaze to the couple sitting about three feet from overflowing garbage. Their tongues are shoved so far down each other's throats that I'm not sure if they're making out or if one is attempting to resuscitate the other.

Good for them.

"I think I'll take the wall," she answers quickly, nodding toward the blank white spot near the windows.

"Good call."

I follow her as she drags her carry-on through the rows of people, lifting it over the kid hunched over his iPad on the floor. I'm not ashamed to admit that I watch her hips sway back and forth, her red hair blowing as we move under the heat vent above us. She's wearing a black, puffy coat over her tiny frame and tall brown boots that zip up over her calves. The majority of her body is covered, but I still can't seem to look away.

When she reaches the open space, she drops her three gift bags between her feet and leans an arm against the wall. I catch up to her, mirroring her stance, my shoulder settling half a foot above hers.

"So, are you going home?" she asks, unzipping her jacket.

I pick at the lid of my coffee cup, suddenly very aware that in a matter of seconds I'll finally be able to see what she's hiding underneath her layers. "Sort of," I say calmly despite the anticipation rushing through me. "I'm going to my parents' house, but I wouldn't call it home."

"Tell me about it," she groans with a roll of her eyes. "Same."

I should question her on it—ask what *she* means by that. But as her jacket slides off her shoulders, all I can do is follow the pattern of lace on the neckline of her flowy white shirt. It hovers over a pair of dark denim and cascades down past her wrists in wide sleeves like damn angel wings. The stark white stands out even more against her freckled skin and red hair, the two colors mixing with the green from her eyes in the perfect Christmas combo.

I'm screwed.

"I'm, uh..." I clear my throat as she lays her jacket over the handle of her suitcase, crossing her arms over her chest and hiding my latest distraction. "Originally from Canada," I finish. "But a few years before I signed with the Flames, my family moved to Barksdale."

She nods as she wraps her long wavy hair around her fist and tosses it behind her. I try not to picture doing the same, but *damn...*

I'm only human.

"Like the uh, tree... not the dog," I continue, shaking my mind of the image.

Her brows slowly fall together as she stares at me, confused.

"The *Bark* in Barksdale..."

"Oh," she draws out. "Got it."

Her tone seems genuine, but she may just be doing a great job at hiding her real reaction. That joke usually lands... but the combination of the cinnamon smell that wafted toward me when she tossed her hair and the mindset I was in before our interaction has me off my game.

"I'm from Frostpine Falls," she says, saving me from the moment. "Also like the tree."

I smile wider than I should, taking in my last sip of coffee in an attempt to hide it at least a little. Nellie lets out the start of a giggle before it morphs into a deep inhale.

"It's really small. Like *really* small. And basically the bane of my existence, so... "

"Oh, so does that explain the relief over being stuck in this crowded airport with me and a few thousand other people forty-eight hours before Christmas?"

She raises her brows as she purses her lips. "Pretty much. Frostpine Falls is everything stereotypical about a small town. Everybody knows everybody's business, people rarely leave, and Christmas... well, Christmas is like an Olympic sport."

"Is it?" I ask, intrigued.

She holds her hand out to me. "Hi, I'm Nellie from Frostpine Falls. Red hair, green eyes, full name Noelle Joy Winters."

"You're kidding," I deadpan.

"I'm not. I live on Evergreen Drive, my house smells like sugar cookies all year round, and I have one younger brother—Kris."

I stare at her as it all sinks in.

"Kris," she repeats bluntly.

"As in Kringle?" I ask in pieces.

She points a finger in my direction. "That's the one."

A chuckle escapes my lips as I bring my arms across my chest. "I think I love your town."

Nellie, who looks not one bit amused by my reaction, rolls her eyes playfully. "You're joking, right?"

I arch a brow. "Noelle Joy—I never joke about jubilation."

"Oh, that's right," she says, huffing out a laugh. "Yeah, you know what? That actually tracks perfectly with what I know about you."

I lick my lips, adjusting my stance and squinting in her direction. Nellie's eyes grow wide, and her arms finally fall back to her sides, her sleeves slinking back over her wrists.

Still an angel.

"I just mean from interviews and the games and stuff," she clarifies. "I swear I'm not a creep."

I smile at her use of my previous statement, half-amused and half turned on as hell.

"I'm actually just so used to being around famous people," she continues over-explaining.

Now my eyebrows shoot up as I tilt my head, not supplying her the same rescue she gave me just moments ago. Watching her squirm is kind of cute.

"Not like that. I'm not *friends* with famous people. We don't hang out or anything. Just working for Liam and having been at the school where a lot of well-known people in Golden City send their kids, I—"

"Nellie," I finally jump in. "I knew what you meant."

She exhales heavily. "Sorry, I'm all thrown off. I think my brain's still on overdrive from everything." She gestures around the gates, and I chuckle as she brings her first two fingers to her forehead.

"I get it," I say. "I feel the same way. This isn't how I thought the airport situation would go." She looks like she might ask why, but I don't feel like ruining this moment. "But now I need to hear this," I say instead. "What is it you know about me?"

Her lips part, then fall closed again as her shoulders slump forward. She waves a hand in front of me, gesturing to what I assume is my entire being, like that's supposed to explain it. When I don't speak, her head falls back.

"You know, you're like..." She looks at me again and wiggles her palm once more. "Everyone knows you. You have a presence."

I know exactly what she's saying, but this is just too good. "A presence?"

"Yeah," she nods, more comfortable now. "You're a big personality—fun, spontaneous, adorable, sil—"

Her cheeks turn the perfect shade of pink as she pauses mid-sentence.

"Adorable, huh?" I ask, throwing my hands on my hips and looking myself up and down.

She scrunches up her face trying to mask her amusement as annoyance. "Like a puppy," she clarifies.

I laugh. "Oh, so *now* we're talking dogs." Nellie runs her tongue over her top teeth, and I follow the movement like my cat Sid with a laser pointer. "And you are *not* a puppy. Is that what you're saying?" I ask when her lips close again.

"More like a wolf."

"You don't look dangerous to me," I quip more seriously than I mean to. She had this whole grumpy thing going on at first, but her clothes, the gifts, her aura—talk about a presence.

I don't buy it for a second.

Nellie's throat moves up and down as she blinks hard. "I've just put off going home for a long time now. But Kris asked me to come back for the holidays this year. I think he's looking for someone to drive him around over break more than anything, honestly. But my boss found out and bought me my ticket, so... I sort of feel like I have to go."

I picture what I've learned about Liam from our few interactions, and I definitely believe it. Nellie pulls a piece of hair over her shoulder and watches it twist as she twirls it around her finger.

"That was nice of him."

"He's also very puppy-like," she says, glancing up at me.

We both laugh, her face already brighter than before.

"Well, if it helps, I'm actually dreading going home too," I admit.

"Is your town also a mile wide and awful?"

I blow a breath through my lips. "No, it's actually pretty big and mostly decent."

"Do you hate Christmas?"

"Obviously not."

"Your family then? Are they the worst?"

There's a slight pang in my chest at the word, but I swallow it down. "No... we're super close."

She turns her lips in and nods slowly. "Mhmm, so, what's the problem then?"

I take a deep breath, buying myself an extra second. "I, uh... "

In perfect timing, Nellie lets out a huge yawn, her hand flying to her mouth. "God, sorry," she says, her voice muffled by her palm. "I think I'm crashing from the chaos."

A wave of relief washes over me in the form of an out—and an excuse for a refill. "We can go find some coffee if you want."

I hold my breath as Nellie considers my question, her eyes wandering around the space as if she's deciding if my offer is better than our current situation. "Yeah, sure," she finally says.

I smile and nod, pushing off of the wall.

"Or something stronger," she adds as I reach for her carry-on, her gaze stuck on the sea of people. "And maybe food."

I peer down at her, holding out her jacket. She takes it and puts her green eyes on me. "That can be arranged."

3

Nellie

"Okay, maybe getting stuck in the airport isn't better than going home. At least on the plane I could get a drink and a bag of mini pretzels."

I look one more time around the flooded food court area, each line miles long, and every seat taken at the tables. At this point, I'd settle for one of those prepackaged mystery meat sandwiches they sell at the kiosks next to old magazines and extra batteries. But even those were wiped clean when we passed them on our way here.

Brett slides his backpack from his shoulder and unzips the front pocket. For a minute I forgot I was with a professional athlete—it's as if we're all one and the same when you're trapped in a public space. But the Flames logo outlined in bright yellow stitching across the top of his bag and the number seven underneath it remind me we're not.

"Shit, sorry. I thought I might have a protein bar in here or something."

I sigh, clicking and re-clicking the button on the handle of my suitcase for the hundredth time. "Can't you play your *I'm Brett Burns* card and slide into line somewhere? Maybe flirt with a girl or two for a coffee and some chicken sandwiches?"

His eyebrows raise as he tilts his head back and forth considering my suggestion as an unsettling pit sinks in my stomach. "Technically... yeah, I absolutely could. I've done way more for far less."

He stares at me straightfaced as a list of things he could have possibly done—and for what—runs through my head. I'm not surprised when most of them include doing *something* with *someone,* and it heats my chest just a little with either lust or jealousy.

Maybe both.

"But I'm honestly not really in the headspace for the Burns' Effect right now."

I squint, trying to pull an explanation—or definition—out of him. When he offers nothing, I respond. "Okay, there is *definitely* something to unpack with everything about that sentence."

"Well, that's what we're trying to get to, right? So, we'll figure something out."

He scans the room, his eyes bouncing around as he takes it all in—analyzes it. They dart in one direction, and the corners of his lips turn upward. Then, they land somewhere else across the room, and his smile grows to reach the dimples that I have a sudden need to draw.

"Follow me," is all he says, and I'm surprised at how quickly I snap my carry-on handle back into place and take off after him.

I walk behind him, taking in his height—and his ass—for the first real time. I knew I was right about his presence even from the start—the *Burns' Effect.* I've seen it countless times on Liam's TV and the few occasions where I may or may not have stalked a few players' Instagrams—the Flames social media manager at the start of the season really knew what she was doing. But I didn't realize that so much of it actually has nothing to do with his goofy personality or on-ice antics.

Brett Burns is an absolute brick wall. He's at least 6'4", with broad shoulders and tree-trunk thighs, and he stands tall and strong like the defenseman he is. Right now, he's leading me only God knows where with quick energy and a powerful authority, and I'm not even at risk of being slammed into glass—I hope.

I can see why his teammates feel safe behind him and why I was so eager to trail him. Brett is a tank—physically, of course—but I also feel protected with him just inches away.

Where was he on my Uber ride over?

"Sit," he commands as he comes to a stop.

I all but crash into him—again—but I pull myself from my mental discovery just in time to catch myself. When I do, that one word hits me right in my core, a heat traveling further south than I'd like to admit.

Maybe I'm more dog than wolf after all.

"Please," he adds quickly with a smile, replacing the sex-god he somehow became with three simple letters with Golden-Retriever-Brett once again.

I finally look past him at a now-open couch of sorts that sits facing the food court. There's still a soda bottle and an empty bag of chips resting on the side table next to it, but Brett quickly sweeps them up.

"I'll be back," he says, walking away.

I hesitate, pulled to follow him again like a puppy on a lead, but shake the image of anything around my neck in Brett's presence. Instead, I plop onto the thick brown leather. The gift bags fall from my elbow onto the spot next to me, and I remember that there's chocolate in one of these bags for Kris.

I shake the realization and resist diving into the snack like I want to. If I did, not only would I be out a present, but with my luck today, I'd end up wearing it or have brown teeth and sticky fingers for when Brett finally gets back.

Instead, I use the moment to people-watch. It's one of my favorite things about living in the city. Sitting down on a bench and sketching those nearby is so unsatisfying in Frostpinc Falls. There's just no excitement in seeing the same handful of people I would have seen anywhere else in town. There's no fun in making up stories about the couple across the street. I already know it's Holly and Clara from high school on their way to the diner because it's Saturday, and where else would they be headed but for their cinnamon roll cappuccinos and warm buttered biscuits?

Not in Golden City, though.

Here, everyone gets their own story. The girl with the floppy beanie pulling a dog in a cart is headed to a holiday market the next state over to sell her handsewn quilts and oversized scarves. The older gentleman wearing a t-shirt and shorts is on his way to an island somewhere to spend the week alone. He's not lonely, though—this is his dream. His business finally took off this year, and he's cashing in on his lifelong plan to spend Christmas under sunshine and palm trees.

Then, there's the man in the quarter-zip sweater with sweat on his brow. He's pacing the space in front of the gift shop, burning off his built-up nervous energy over flying across the country to propose to his long-distance girlfriend after two crawling years apart.

No, in Golden City everyone gets a narrative. Some I don't know at all, and some I can partially piece together. Like this one. The guy with the big smile and stained peacoat, using one giant hand to balance two coffee cups and hugging the other to his chest, a pile of snacks tucked inside.

I don't know his story—not exactly. I think I might—the jokester hockey player full of optimism and a bubbling personality. But there's something else there that's tinting that slightly. A weak shadow cast over him, but there all the same.

Brett steps closer to me, his eyes on the mound of carbs and sugar.

"Okay, what kind of sorcery did you have to do to get all of that?" I ask, standing to meet him. "Did you use the Burns' Effect after all?"

Brett wiggles his brows up and down, a sly smirk on his face. Once again, a twinge of something close to annoyance over his flirting with someone for my sustenance hits me differently than I'd expect it to.

"Scratch that," I blurt. "I don't think I want to know."

"You sure?" Brett licks his lips, and suddenly I'm not sure of anything. He drops the snacks onto the end table where the last occupant's trash once was and shoves his hands into his jean pockets. "Because I could give you details. Tell you how I used my hands. How I slowly pressed my fingers to all the right spots. Waited for that sound that told me it was time—time to shove inside and get what I came for..."

He holds my gaze, his eyes low, his breathing steady, and I hold on to every damn word he says. My brain is fully aware that this is some kind of joke, but my body's on edge for the story's climax—or mine.

My lips part, my heart beating at the pace of the flowing crowd around us, but it's like we're the only two in the room as my vision tunnels in his direction. I swallow the need that's built up under my tongue as I find myself leaning toward him—closer. Drawn to him.

Just when I think I might fall into him all over again, this time for a different reason, Brett pops back up like a spring. "And that's what happened when I found the vending machines over there by the bathrooms," he says cheerfully, looking over his shoulder at the row of metal I now hate with a passion.

I drag myself back and wipe the metaphorical—and actual—drool dripping from my lips before he turns back around. I assume, at first, that something about the angst of going home, the current situation, or my lack of caffeine must have caused my full-body dysfunction just now. But then I realize, nope.

It's just him.

Damn, the Burns' Effect is strong.

"Well, thanks," I sing in overcompensation. I grab one coffee from his hand and nearly burn my tongue chugging it before I realize it tastes like absolute ass. "Oh my God." I choke down the sip before looking at the cup like it might reveal itself as actual poison.

"Did I mention that the coffee *also* came from a vending machine?" Brett winces.

"Definitely not," I manage.

He raises his cup and takes a quick whiff. "Sorry. I thought it might be worth a shot."

"I mean, don't let me stop you," I say, setting mine on the table. "Go for it."

"Yeah, I think I'm good." He shakes his head and sets his cup next to mine.

Brett gestures to the couch, and only now do I realize how small it is—now that his large frame is supposed to fit on it with mine. Sliding over as far as I can, I drop my gift bags to the floor and twist my body so I'm up on one cheek, allowing him as much room as possible.

He sits down, doing the same, his hips turned either creating more space or so he can fully face me. "So, you said you worked at a school?"

I'm taken aback by the question, not because it's odd but because he remembered from that one rambling thought. "Yeah, I used to run the after-care program at the elementary school on the west side. That's where I met Ruthie and Liam, actually. With his baseball schedule, pickup right at dismissal was sometimes tricky, so either he or Levi would get her later."

Brett's face lights up at his coach's name. Levi is the Flames' head coach. He is also the brother of Liam—Golden City Gator's shortstop, single dad, and my current boss.

"Ruthie loved it," I continue. "She would hang with me, and we'd talk about life while she got through her math homework and I planned the schedule for the next week's activities. She came in waves, being that with their schedules so opposite, Liam or Levi could usually get her from school. But we bonded over art and wagers."

"Your usual combo," he jokes sarcastically.

"Ruthie plays a mean Tic-Tac-Toe."

He purses his lips and nods.

"In June, though, Ruthie finished fourth grade and graduated from elementary school. Her Uncle Levi, as I'm sure you know, also got engaged. Liam started realizing that with less help and middle school rigor, Ruthie might need more than a little after-school homework care."

"So, Monte Sr. poached you?"

"Well, I mean... I wasn't in love with where I was, I just..."

Brett tilts his chin down and gives me a knowing look.

"He basically poached me, yeah."

"Savage." Brett smiles and reaches back toward the table. "Salty or sweet?"

I hear his question, but my mind is stuck on the way his jacket pulls tight across his back as it twists, his bicep bulging underneath the wool without even flexing. It's only when the fabric settles as he turns back around that I realize I haven't actually answered.

"Oh, uh... sweet."

"Good choice." He extends his arm again, but this time, I force myself to look at the faded leather on the three inches of couch between us. "PopTarts, gummy bears, Twizzlers, or M&Ms?"

I'm tempted to answer chocolate until I remember my thoughts from earlier. "Twizzlers," I say instead. "Please."

Brett grabs the pack of red licorice and a rainbow bag of gummies. I take the Twizzlers from his hand and tear the package open, hoping the candy will fuel both my exhaustion and my hunger.

"Are you a peeler or do you eat them attached like they're all one bar?" he asks, ripping open the bag of bears.

I pause with my thumb and forefinger wrapped around one Twizzler, ready to pull it apart from the others. "Wait, what? Who eats them all together?"

His eyes grow wide as they dart to the open bag in his hand. "Uh... no one. That'd be so weird." He glances up at me in amusement, his one shoulder shrugged.

"Stop. You do not."

"I do."

"You're an animal, Brett Burns."

The smile on his face melts my heart and panties simultaneously. "An adorable puppy, if I recall."

I roll my eyes playfully, nodding toward the handful of candies in his hand. "If you were a gummy bear, which color would you be?"

"Orange," he says with no hesitation.

I'm surprised by his definitiveness. "Not red?" I ask, taking a bite of my candy. "That would have been my guess."

"Nah," he says, digging into the bag and picking out a him-colored gummy. "Orange is fun—bright and energizing." He pops it into his mouth. "But it's also steady—dependable, strong."

I laugh as we both chew our sweets. "That's unexpectedly deep."

"Yeah, well," he chews his candy. "A teammate's been teaching me a thing or two about poetry."

I nod, impressed, as he searches for another one of the same. When he finds one, he holds it up, inspecting it. "But it's true. Orange is a solid flavor. People like it. But it's not the favorite—not the one your eyes go to first. That's the—"

"Red," I finish for him.

He looks over the gummy, but despite his words, he doesn't seem sad. He smirks genuinely, then winks in my direction. "Exactly," he says, tossing it into the air and catching it between his lips.

I shake my head as I finally swallow my bite. Brett's words wash over me as he plucks a red gummy bear from the pack and shows it off. I stare at it, trying to answer my own question. What color would I be?

For a second, I wonder if some from back home would say red. I left—escaped. I stand out because I moved on from our little corner of the world and am building my own life for myself.

But then it hits me that others would say the opposite. The people Frostpine Falls remember—the ones their eyes go to first—they're the ones that stayed. The big fish in the small pond who played it safe. To them, I'm the clear one. The mystery flavor that they don't quite understand. The one who isn't sure if it wants to be sweet or tart—that doesn't fit into their neat little rainbow.

Brett holds another red one in the air, ready to throw it. I part my lips for him, feeling about as ridiculous as I probably look, but it doesn't stop me.

This doesn't happen in Frostpine Falls. You don't have unexpected meet-cutes or full conversations about colors of sugar. You don't casually—and almost fatally—run into an NHL player who chooses you of all people to waste their time with.

That's what this city means to me. That's what leaving meant to me. Opportunities. Dreams. Airport adventures. And so, even if no one else agrees—even if nothing has come from it yet—that's why I'm here.

And as I catch the candy in my mouth, I realize this is the exact reminder that I needed.

4

Brett

"**F**eeling any better?"

Nellie pulls the second s'mores PopTart from the shiny foil and breaks it down the middle, biting off the top of one half. "Honestly, I felt better the second I heard there was more time between me and Frostpine Falls." She takes another bite and exhales heavily. "But this helps too."

I smile as I hold a red and green M&M together and pop them both into my mouth. "Good."

"Thank you, by the way," she adds. "For the sugar rush."

I nod. "So, what is it about going back that made you all..." I try to choose my words wisely. I'm clearly comfortable around the girl already, but that doesn't change that we quite literally ran into each other for the first time approximately forty-six minutes ago.

"Grouchy?" she offers.

I consider her answer before suggesting a different one. "How about tense?"

She purses her lips, and I finally allow myself to really take them in like I've wanted to since her first bite.

Damn.

"I'll take it."

"Is it really that bad?" I ask.

She licks said lips, her gaze dropping to the floor as she thinks—or maybe contemplates how much to share. "It's not. My family's there and a couple of friends. The Christmas thing is fun when it isn't totally cringy, but people are judgy and relentless." She sighs. "And there's this guy..."

My heart sinks slightly, and I try not to show it, but I can feel my jaw growing tighter by the second. It's my own fault for thinking a girl like her wouldn't have someone—or be hung up on somebody that didn't know what they lost. I curse myself mentally for once again growing instantly attached and think about what Helen would say.

Following our steps, I pause, take a breath, and remind myself that feelings aren't facts. I start weeding through what I actually know about Nellie and what I've already made up in my head when she cuts off my thinking with three simple words.

"Not like that."

My shoulders instantly relax.

Chill out, Burnsey, eh?

"I can't stand him, actually," she continues. "But he exists, and he's there. And his entire being drives me crazy."

"I assume he's an ex?"

"Yeah, from high school. We broke up when I decided I wanted to leave Frostpine Falls. He didn't understand. In his mind, we'd get married and take over the bed-and-breakfast that his family owns—him handling the business side and me managing the hospitality. We'd get married, buy a home somewhere between the houses we grew up in, and live happily ever after in the same place we spent our first eighteen years."

"And I take it you didn't see it that way?"

"One place—one small ass town—as the setting to everything? No way. How boring is that? The same roads, the same houses, the same people—the same backdrop to where we were born, where we met, and where we'd die."

"Wow."

Nellie rolls her eyes and adjusts, pulling one leg under the other to face me. Her knee grazes my thigh... not that I notice.

"Okay, that's dramatic. But you get what I'm saying."

I set my candy in my lap and drape my arm over the back of the couch. "So, *he's* why you don't go home?"

"God no," she says quickly. "Well, yes... but not *only* him. Going home is just a reminder that I took a risk that hasn't necessarily paid off. Everyone already thought I was crazy for leaving. But then knowing that I never actually made anything of myself out here..." Her brows rise, and her cheeks light up, her words trailing off as if she didn't mean to say that last part out loud.

"I bet Ruthie would disagree with you," I say casually. Her eyes shoot to mine as the color in her face slowly returns to normal. "And Liam."

Her gaze falls to her lap as she nibbles at her bottom lip. "Sure, I know. I just... this wasn't really my plan, ya know?"

My instincts form the next natural question on the tip of my tongue—*then what was your plan?* But I can sense exactly how she's feeling. Lately I've taken on the weight of change and unexpectedness, and despite my curiosity, I decide against pulling it from her.

"What's in the bags?"

She tilts her head, and I nod toward the gifts on the floor.

"Oh."

She peers between her legs, and her hair falls in front of her profile. It's the same shade of copper that lights up the city when the sun rises or sets between the buildings. I almost reach out and touch it—not to be weird, but just because it's so beautiful it almost doesn't seem real. But I don't need Helen to tell me how *much* that is—how unsettling it could be to someone who isn't full throttle like I am.

"Some chocolate from that place on Ninth for Kris, a candle for my mom, and a Golden City snow globe for my dad. He collects them."

"Snow globes?"

"Yep, and he leaves them out all year long. Most of them are from different stores or boutiques in Frostpine Falls considering he doesn't really leave. But I try to find one to bring back everywhere I go." She grabs the silky ribbon on the navy bag covered in snowmen and glances at the white tissue paper hanging out the top like it might be looking back. She dips her hand in and pushes it aside, peering in without actually pulling the present out. "It hit me when I was last-minute shopping that I haven't gotten him one from G.C. since I graduated college."

"Why not?"

"I haven't been home."

I arch a brow. "For Christmas?"

"At all."

I pull my head back, surprised by her statement and how simple she makes it seem. "How long has it been?"

Nellie drags her bottom lip between her teeth. "Like three years."

"Wow," I say quickly. My mom and dad's faces flash before my eyes—their smiles a mile long each time their cab pulls up to my place. "That's a long time. I see my parents a few times each month."

Nellie's face almost falls, but her lips curl up at the last minute. I still see her, though—and the tint of sorrow in her eyes. "Do they visit you, or do you visit them?"

"They visit me mostly. I fly them out for our big games or if we have away trips anywhere cool." My words slow as the rest tumbles out. "They sort of love to travel..."

She laughs sadly as she shakes her head. "So, basically the opposite of mine. They came to G.C. to drop me off at school and haven't been back since."

Before I can stop myself, my palm lands on the knee she still has resting near my leg. "I'm sorry."

Her eyes follow my hand as I pull it back. "For what?"

"That you haven't seen them." I cross my arms over my chest as a wave of my own grief washes over me. "That's hard."

"It is, but we FaceTime. And Kris has been here with a friend a few times. They came up for a couple Flames' games, actually."

I sit up straighter, grinning smugly. "In that case... you're welcome." She smiles genuinely for the first time since I asked about the presents, and I feel unnecessarily rewarded. "That's cool though," I say, my chest full. "That you're close with your brother. My little sister is like my favorite person in the world."

Nellie grins. "How old is she?"

"She just turned eighteen," I say, sucking in air.

She blows out a breath. "Poor girl."

My neck snaps forward dramatically. "Poor *girl*? Poor me! By Canadian law, she's legal now. And I, by the laws of nature, am screwed."

She giggles angelically, somehow looking at me more intensely than before. I hold her gaze, allowing her eye contact to fully sink in, memorizing the ring of deep emerald that runs along the outer layer. She stares back for another few moments, a comfortable silence falling between us. Then, inhaling slowly, her eyes drift back to the floor.

"I guess both of our parents like a good age gap then."

I swallow, turning away from her to face the crowd. Dropping my forearms onto the tops of my thighs, I lean forward. "We're half-siblings, actually." I glance over at Nellie as she nods easily. "But I've never considered her any less my sister."

She drops her leg and puts two feet back on the floor. "That's sweet."

An all too familiar guilt floods my gut—the uncomfortable friend that's been lingering for these past few weeks. Rather than let it settle, I try to remember my responsibility in everything that's happened. And remind myself, that's what I'm on my way to handle.

Somehow.

"Hey, what do you say we go do something fun?"

Nellie whips her head in my direction. "In an airport?"

I shrug. "Sure, why not?" Peering over at her, I smile just from seeing hers. "It's an adventure, remember?"

She glances around and takes in the three small boys rolling around underneath their parents' feet and the older man snoring across from us with his shoes off and his belly out. "It's something alright."

"Then, what do you say? Should we find some fun?"

She considers it another moment before slapping her hands on her knees and popping up. "Let's do it."

I unzip my backpack and throw the extra snacks inside before standing to meet her. "Cool," is all I say.

"Okay, that's the one." Nellie looks back in the mirror at the floppy Golden City bucket hat resting on her head. She rolls her eyes at me in the reflection, the heavy yellow fabric somehow less gaudy on her. "I'm serious," I say. "You're getting it."

She laughs, taking it off and putting it back on the rack beside her. "I'm definitely not."

"Oh, come on. Where's the *joy*, Noelle?" I emphasize the three-letter word that doubles as her middle name.

"I'll tell you what..." She turns to me with her hands on her hips. "I'll get the hat if you buy those." She points to a pair of tiny, red cotton shorts that say *Flames* across the butt.

"These?" I walk over to the row of sports-themed clothing and pull them off the front of the rack. "Joke's on you. I already own these."

"Stop," she snorts.

I turn around and hold them up to my ass, the whole pair barely covering one cheek. "You clearly underestimate how ridiculous I am."

Suddenly, her face grows serious. "Wait... I don't know if I believe you. Do you really?"

I spin back around, hanging the insanely small shorts back where they started. "I guess you'll never know."

"That's just cruel."

"Yeah, well, so is denying the world a view of you in that cool yellow hat."

She narrows her eyes in my direction before stepping over to the jewelry display. "Warm," she says.

"What?" I walk over to her, scanning the rows of stud earrings in every color on the side of the spinning rack closest to me.

"Yellow's a warm color, so that hat is in fact *not* cool in any way."

"First of all," I slowly spin the rectangular rack so that the next side is turned toward each of us. "If we're being technical, I actually knew that. Flames—fire—red, orange, yellow." She looks over at me sideways, the lower half of a sun necklace still hanging off a hook, draped over her hand. "We're not just warm. We're burnin' hot, baby."

She laughs as she drops the gold chain, her fingers moving to the edges of the stand.

"And second... Picasso... I didn't know you were some kind of artist."

"That's because I'm not," she throws back. She turns the display so I'm now looking at the necklaces, metal clinking gently in the silence.

"Okay, well, *I'm* not out here throwing around facts about the color wheel, so I just thought—"

"You thought wrong." She cuts me off, but her tone's not harsh—just hurried. Her hands fly to a piece of jewelry, and she plucks it off its hook. She dangles what I can now see is an airplane charm between two fingers, then holds it up to me. "Now, *this* I think I'll get."

I try to read her expression, but the excitement over the tiny silver plane masks her previous discontent. "Do you have other charms?"

"No."

"A bracelet at least?"

"Nope." She laughs. "But that's okay. Maybe that'll be my thing. I'll collect charms wherever I go."

"Your snow globes," I say.

She looks at me and smiles softly. "Exactly."

I shake the thought that maybe one day she'll wear a Barksdale charm—or even better, one from home—and nod. I grab it from her grasp, brushing past her and snagging the bucket hat from the hook she placed it on. "Then I need something too."

I move toward the register, placing both items on the counter. The cashier, an older woman with her hair tied back, gray pieces pulled out to frame her face, looks at the two of us as she scans each one.

"His and her souvenirs?" she asks sweetly.

"Something like that," Nellie responds, looking at me. It's not a confession of love—in fact, it's barely an answer—but my breath catches all the same.

I scan my card as the woman packs up our things, then I take the gift shop bag from her. "Thank you."

"Safe travels, you two."

I hand the bag to Nellie. "Thanks for this," she says, pulling the charm out from the bottom.

She slings her backpack forward and slides it into the small zipper pocket, then reaches back into the bag and pulls out my hat. She holds it up, but rather than taking it from her, I lean forward so our faces are merely inches apart.

Dipping my head down, I fix my gaze on the hem of her sleeve that still hangs down to her collarbone. I don't mean to notice, but there's no missing the way her chest now moves up and down in strong waves. I hover there until she drags the hat over my hair.

Standing back up, I keep my eyes down until I finally bring them up to meet hers. "This feels right," I say, adjusting the rim of the hat and ignoring the way her irises darken.

"Yeah," she huffs, swallowing hard and tucking her hair behind her ears. "The hat looks good on you, I must say."

"Oh, I know," I joke back.

But that's not what I meant.

5

Nellie

"Where are we?"

Brett glances around, looking over both shoulders. "I think we're headed toward the international gates."

"Geez, how long have we been walking?" I switch my gift bags to the other arm and shake out my wrist.

"I'm honestly not sure. I've been playing Frogger in my head, just dodging oncoming traffic and trying not to get clipped by a carry-on."

I pull on the handle of my rolling suitcase and gently knock it against the back of his shoe. "You mean, like that?"

He shoots me a faux-evil eye that shouldn't be sexy, and yet it still forces my thighs together. "Just like that." His expression turns playful once again, and I ignore the dimples I know are there that will only further turn me on.

Ever since the gift shop, I can't seem to shake that there's something so special about this guy. He's hot, of course, and has this adorable innocence that pairs perfectly with his puppy dog vibes, but it's more than that.

He seems sweet and sincere and so damn genuine. People see him as goofy and entertaining—I know that from sports news and social media. But there are sides to him that I've caught glimpses of that are funny, sure, and even silly, but are also honest and authentic. Like he really does just radiate happiness.

Girls are taught that broodiness and angst are the pillars of temptation. We watch movies and read books where the hot guy is the moody one. The dark one. The bad boy. But apparently not enough screenwriters or romance authors have met Brett "Sunshine" Burns. His smile and humor could rival tattoos and a gold chain any day of the week.

"Woah, it's getting dark," I say as we walk past a row of windows. "It's been longer than I thought since—"

"Since you attempted to burn me to death with my coffee?"

I glare at him, sucking my teeth. "I was going to say, since we met."

He smiles slyly and glances down at his gold Rolex. "Time flies when you're having an airport adventure."

"Speaking of..."

I grab his arm and pull him toward two surprisingly open chairs along a charging station that grab my attention. His bicep flexes beneath my palm, and I whip around to glare at him. Brett looks at me, confusion etched into his brow, and I realize he didn't purposefully flaunt his muscle—he simply moved his arm.

"You still owe me details," I say, sitting in one of the empty seats, fanning myself from our trek over—and Brett's impeccable physique.

The international gates are quieter than I expected—or maybe just not as loud as the hustle and bustle everywhere else. There are a handful of other people here—reading, sleeping, or scrolling on their phone—but there's enough room to slide our things into the space between us. Brett takes the free chair next to mine, and we both sink into the cushions instantly.

"What do you want to know?"

I unzip my bag and pull my charger from the first pocket. Plugging it into the slot in front of me, I connect my phone and place it on the desk. "Well, you know why *I'm* not thrilled to be flying back home for Christmas. What's your story?"

Brett sighs, shrugging out of his jacket for the first time since our collision. The sweater he has on underneath is simple—tan, cashmere, just tight enough to distract me with a sudden urge to nuzzle into the dip between his chest.

"I'm sort of putting off a conversation."

My gaze flies back to his. "A man of mystery, huh?"

He chuckles awkwardly, leaning forward on the counter. "Not at all, actually. I don't know if you've noticed, but I'm normally the all-in type. Loyal, devoted, affectionate—"

"A puppy, yes. We've covered this."

We both smile until Brett's fades as he runs his hand down his face. "But that means no secrets. I mean, I'm basically incapable." He folds his hands in front of him and watches as he rubs one thumb over the other. "An open book, if you will."

"But that also makes hard conversations worse."

His eyes dart to mine. "Exactly."

He turns to me with a recognition in his eyes and an energy that only comes from feeling understood—like somebody gets it. A feeling I rarely experience in Frostpine Falls.

I mirror him, our knees nearly touching. "So, what is it? Do you secretly hate kittens? Are you quitting hockey? Oh my God..." I scoot my chair back just an inch, leaning in to my usual thoughts. "Did you kill someone?"

"What?" he cries out, his hand on his chest. "Are you serious?" He looks at me genuinely offended.

"Brett, I was just—"

"Of course I don't hate kittens, Nellie." My shoulders sag. "I *have* a cat, thank you very much. And for your information, Sidney Clawsby is an absolute legend."

Brett ticks another box, surprising me yet again. "Sidney Clawsby?"

"Don't act like that's not genius."

I snort out a laugh. "Okay, sorry. Sidney Clawsby—noted. So, what is it then? Did you elope with a stranger you met online? Do you have a couple of kids running around somewhere?" I'm teasing, but there's a very real anxiousness that lingers in my stomach as I hold my breath, waiting for his answer.

"We just established that I can't keep secrets, and you think I have a wife or children that no one knows about?"

A heaviness lifts from my chest that shouldn't have been there in the first place. "Hey, I'm just taking guesses." I rest my chin in my palm. "Ooh, maybe you're actually Canadian royalty and this whole professional hockey player thing is just a cover."

"For what?"

"I don't know... I never said it made sense."

"I'm not royal," he says. Brett looks back down at his hands before his head snaps back up. "But I do look damn good in a crown."

I narrow my eyes.

"Trying to picture it?" he asks.

"No," I admit. "Just trying to figure out when that would have even been discovered."

"Don't ask questions you don't want the answers to, Noelle."

His tone is stern, but he says it jokingly, and yet I still immediately picture him naked.

"Will you just tell me," I beg.

He takes a deep breath and exhales heavily. "Okay, so..."

His voice fades, his words swallowed by a random chorus of French that rings out around us. A pack of college students swarm the gate in *I heart G.C.* t-shirts layered under neutral cardigans and tucked into slim-fit jeans. One of them—with a dark mustache and a rather large receding hairline—holds a phone above his head, instrumentals raining out.

I look at Brett who is staring, stunned, as they cluster together. Girls sway and guys drape their arms over one another's shoulders as they belt out the words of *It's Beginning to Look A Lot Like Christmas* in that unmistakable romantic lilt. They sound great—extremely loud and slightly off-key, but I'm not sure I've ever heard something in French sound ugly.

Brett glances over at me when one of the girls throws her head back as she attempts to hit a high note in harmony. He half-shrugs, watching in either awe or disbelief, a faint smile tugging at his lips.

When the song comes to an end, we both clap gently. Assuming the song is over, I go to comment aloud to Brett, but as I do, the group instantly dives into the next number. I snap my mouth shut as they begin *Blue Christmas,* which is mostly recognizable because the man that starts singing curls one side of his top lip up dramatically as a smooth baritone rolls off his tongue. The group shifts, surrounding us like fish in a bowl, but continues to sing as if we aren't even there.

What is happening?

"Do you think they're some sort of choir?" I ask in a loud whisper, my focus trained on a man so in tune with the lyrics that his eyes are closed as if it's a hymn. No one else seems to notice. They're all in their own worlds, soaking up the vibe.

Brett leans in, clearly unable to hear me over the sweet soulful sound of the soloist.

I sigh, scooting my chair as close to his as our bags will allow. I wave him in, and he sits up further in his chair, bending forward so his ear is by my mouth, our cheeks almost touching. I avoid breathing, mostly because my breath shoots out in too-short spurts in the most noticeable way, but also because the smell of him—musky but almost sweet—threatens to pull me right onto his lap.

I clear my throat of the lust that's caught there. "Do you think they're in a choir or something?" I repeat, my words drifting out in quiet pieces—nowhere as fluid as the chorus surrounding us.

Brett pulls away, tilting his head to look me in the eye, a lazy smile on his lips that I'm tempted to taste. There's a moment where he must be able to read my thoughts, his puppy-dog eyes suddenly darker. "I..." he starts as his gaze dips down to my mouth.

I finally inhale slowly, filling my chest with both air and anticipation as the rest of the singers join in.

Brett's jaw tightens as his mouth falls into a flat line. "I think..." he tries again, his lips nearly touching mine.

I hold steady, ignoring the idea that if this were to happen—if he were to press them to mine right here, right now—that I would essentially be kissing a stranger during a flash mob in the middle of an airport. I'm all but convinced that none of that matters. *This* is why I love it here—new people, ridiculous adventures, first kisses that are somehow sexy and laughable at the same time.

I'm contemplating closing what little gap still sits between us, my heart pounding and adrenaline coursing through my veins, when I'm shoved from the side by a tall lanky man attempting to shake his hips and swivel his legs as if he were Elvis himself.

"Ooh, pardon," he says, his accent heavy. I smile weakly up at him, my blood now hot for an entirely different reason, only to look back and find Brett's dimple on full display.

"I think they're super drunk," he finally finishes, pulling back.

There's a disappointment in my stomach that's all too familiar. It's not just the ache of having wanted to have Brett's lips on mine, but that feeling of being in the perfect place for dreams to come true and, still, it doesn't happen.

"Must be nice," I yell back, bitterness etched in every word.

Brett may notice, or maybe—like the imitation Presley—he has impeccable timing.

"Wait, come on," he says, grabbing my wrist and branding me with a simple touch. "That just gave me an idea."

"Okay..." I drag out, slightly annoyed that *this* was his grand proposal. "I guess Christmas shopping in duty-free beats listening to whatever carol came next." The French production at gate seventeen was funny at first—festive even—but one more song and I might have lost it.

"It's not a gift," he says as he smiles at the woman and takes the sealed bag from the clerk. He unzips his backpack on the counter and slips the two bottles of wine inside.

"You know, for someone who says they can't keep secrets, you're full of 'em today."

Brett laughs as he grabs my hand and pulls me toward the exit. "Give me another minute, and it'll all make sense."

He leads me through oncoming traffic, my gift bags flapping between us. I might usually question why he's guiding me back into the most populated part of the airport, but I can't rip my focus away from how our fingers interlock. When we pass the French students now having a kumbaya moment on the floor, the beginning notes of *Feliz Navidad* pouring from the makeshift speaker, I'm thankful anyway.

We bob and weave another couple of feet, my carry-on only clipping a handful of ankles along the way. I throw out a few *sorry's,* and Brett offers a couple of *excuse me's* as we dodge other people that are still somehow flooding the hallway despite having nowhere to go.

I guess everyone's on a mission to find something to do.

Just when I think we might be heading to the other side of the airport—or maybe the damn moon at this pace—I'm tugged toward a wall with bathrooms to one side and a slightly cracked-open door to the other.

"Are you going to tell me what we're doing or...?"

"Get in," Brett says, nudging my shoulder toward the opening. I comply, falling into the unknown space and yanking my bags in with me.

Where is true-crime Nellie now?

"Brett, what the hell?" The door slams shut behind me followed by a brief moment of darkness. There's a split second where common sense kicks in—this whole Golden Retriever thing could all be an act that he uses to gain women's trust before luring them into—

A dull light kicks on.

"A supply closet?" My eyes wander, adjusting to the change as they trail over brooms, sprays, and a lifetime supply of those useless, brown paper towels.

"I remember seeing it when we were walking by before. I thought it was weird that it was open." Brett whips his backpack around and unzips the pocket.

"You noticed?"

"Of course." He reaches for the bag from duty-free as I stare at him blankly. He pauses. "It's literally my job to notice things, Nellie. It's usually moving pucks or a forward's tell, but sometimes that translates into an unlocked supply closet that may or may not be our only reprieve from airport dwellers or unannounced concerts."

His words sink in as his plan finally hits me. "You're a genius," I say, soaking up both the silence and the stillness in the small, vacant room.

"Obviously," he says bluntly as he rips the plastic open.

"Wait, isn't this against the rules? I thought those bags were sealed for a reason."

He pulls a bottle of white from the top and sets it on the floor by his feet. "Well, Nellie... yes, they are. But we're having ourselves an adventure." He sets the red beside the other and smiles up at me. "I won't tell if you won't."

"Ha!" I cry. "See... you are good at secrets."

6

Brett

"Would you rather accidentally send a nude to your boss or your mom?" I ask, smirking into the lip of my bottle.

Nellie's face twists instantly. "What? Ew." She slouches, her wine sinking further into her lap. "Come on, that's impossible."

I shrug casually, taking a sip from my bottle. "You have to pick one."

"I don't want to," she whines. "Liam is cool, but how awkward would that be? And my mom? No... just no."

I grin. "Guess you gotta drink then."

"This isn't fair."

I lean in, clinking my bottle to hers. "Those are the rules, remember?"

She rolls her eyes. "What I remember is you making this sound fun, but so far, all you've given me are these bogus choices."

"Bogus, eh?" I shoot her a smile, and she nods in faux annoyance. "Drink."

Nellie sighs, swigging straight from the bottle the same way I have all night. We've been at this since the second we unscrewed the metal lids and sat cross-legged on the supply closet floor, neither of us actually following the rules.

"I think I forgot we're only supposed to drink when we don't want to answer," she admits, holding up her half-empty bottle.

I mirror her, the faintly visible line in mine not any higher. "Same," I laugh. "Guess it's been a longer day than I thought."

For a second, my smile fades as I pick at the label wrapped around the glass. I still haven't told her the reason I don't want to go home, and she hasn't asked again since we were interrupted last time. Part of me hopes she doesn't, saving me and our adventure. But another part of me—an embarrassingly big part—wishes she would.

She tilts her head. "Would you rather chase your dreams or play it safe?"

The change of pace grabs my attention, and my eyes snap to hers. "I'm a professional athlete, Nellie. My career—my *dream*—could literally end tomorrow. I run at it full speed every time I touch the ice."

She nods, taking another sip of her white. "That's fair."

I drain a gulp of my red, then tip my chin in her direction. "What about you?"

She nibbles at her lip, a heat flushing her cheeks from either the wine or something deeper. There's a moment when I think she'll answer, but she doesn't. After another beat of silence, I lean in, asking again without words this time.

"I left Frostpine Falls to do art," she confesses.

"Is that not allowed there?" I deadpan.

A snort rips from her throat before she can stop herself.

"Wow," I chuckle, my eyes growing wide. "I was going to apologize for letting that slip, but *that* reaction? Totally worth it."

She swats at my arm, smothering a smile. "It's allowed," she answers before her face falls flat again. "But nothing would have ever come of it—nothing ever does there. I knew that going to college in a big city gave me a better shot, so that's what I did. I studied psychology and spent every spare second drawing the city. I sat on benches in the park, in booths in restaurants, and at the counter of a dozen coffee shops."

"Drippy's?" I ask excitedly.

She narrows her eyes. "Obviously."

She smiles as she brings the bottle to her lips. My first thought is that the way they mold around the top is a work of art in itself. My second is that I've had too much wine. I shake the thought from my head and go back to listening intently as she continues talking, running her thumb along the inseam of her jeans.

"Anyway," she starts again, her eyes drifting from mine. "I had so much fun really leaning into it—truly falling in love. I was determined to prove art was enough, ya know? So, I applied to galleries, pitched mural ideas to every business with a blank wall—even tried starting a club during the after-school program." She shrugs and shakes her head as her next words are no big deal. "Nothing ever came of it. Something always got in the way—I was denied, declined, told money was too tight or interest too low. I thought after college it might all click into place—that something might stick that would allow me to devote real time to it—but that never happened."

Her eyes trail back to mine for the first time since she started explaining, but when she meets my gaze—steadfast on her—they dart away again. "Sorry, that was a lot. Wine either makes me chatty or slee—"

"Don't be sorry," I cut in, setting my bottle aside and resting my chin in my hands. "Keep going."

She tries to wave me off, but I can tell she's holding back tears. "No, that's it really," she says through a deep inhale. "I don't draw as much anymore—just stopped holding my breath. I'm probably not good enough to make it more than a hobby, and that's okay. It's just... I came for psychology and art, and well... I'm not really using either." Her voice wavers. "But I've learned to enjoy the other opportunities here. I love my job with Ruthie, and every day in the city brings something different. I could never say that about the cage I'd be in back at home."

"It's still hard, though," I reassure her.

She presses her lips into a flat line. "It's just not what I pictured."

Her words hit me unexpectedly, and a silence falls between us. I decide I should tell her—I have to—and the words practically crawl from my throat. I attempt to hold them back—here we are, strangers, and I'm preparing to dump this on her while sitting wedged between a mop bucket and an extra garbage bin.

But before I can stop myself, I do.

"My dad came back into my life a few months ago for the first time in nearly two decades," I blurt.

Her face floods with confusion. "Wait, I thought you were close with your parents?"

"With my mom and stepdad, yeah. Tom's been around since I was in kindergarten. He's the only real father I've ever known. I don't think of Bailey as my half-sister because in my mind, her dad's my dad too, ya know? Always has been—at least in the ways that matter."

Her face softens, and somewhere in the green of her eyes, I find the courage to continue. "But my biological father sent me a letter at the end of the summer." I huff out a sigh disguised as a laugh. "The first piece of mail—the first form of communication—from my real dad in nearly twenty years. I didn't know what to do with it at first. I was confused, surprised—pissed. I had spent the first few years of my twenties finally working through all of this with my therapist and—"

"You see a therapist?" She interrupts, curiosity etched on her forehead. "Sorry," she backtracks quickly. "It's just... *you* see a therapist?"

I arch a brow. "I do."

She stares at me as if she's trying to decide whether I'm telling the truth. "Are you being serious? Or are you just saying that because I told you I was a psych major in school?"

I tilt my chin down and lean in, my hand to my chest. "Nellie, I would never joke about my professional relationship with Helen. That woman is a saint."

Her eyes seem to darken, and the idea that she's turned on by that does something to me.

"Go on," she says, her voice softer than before.

"So, he writes me this letter saying he's different now—sober, grounded—and that despite what I might think, he's spent the last twenty years missing me and following my career online and in the papers." I stretch one leg out and pull the other knee up, leaning back on my hands. Her eyes drop to the small space between our thighs, and mine follow.

"What did you do?" she asks, pulling me back to the moment.

"Well, nothing at first," I sigh. "I took time to process—to decide how I felt and what I wanted to come from it, if anything." Nellie listens intently, and I feel myself growing closer to her even though I haven't moved.

"But the letters kept coming—filled with apologies and promises—one a week until I finally answered."

She unfolds her legs, leaving one bent in and straightening the other so it lays next to me. "You wrote back? What did you say?"

I suck my teeth, mindlessly finding the frayed edge at the hem of her jeans and holding onto it like a lifeline. "The truth."

Nellie holds my gaze, not like she's waiting or even fully invested. But like she's seeing me in a new light than before.

"I told him I didn't know *what* to say. That I was mad at him for leaving—for hurting me and my mom like he did. I told him I was glad that he was doing well because, in reality, I am too, but that I wasn't sure what him coming back around would look like. My mom was a mess when he left, *that* I remember. And there were plenty of scars that he left in the rearview. She and my... Tom... are so good together. She finally got the life she deserved. *I'm* happy, and Bailey has never known anything except our small little family." I exhale heavily. "Just because she's an adult now on paper, doesn't mean she won't always be my little sister. I don't want to throw a wrench in her life like this."

She nods in silent understanding, and her foot falls inward naturally. When her ankle lands against my hip, neither of us makes any attempt to separate, our proximity only mirroring our conversation.

"This has to be so hard on you—him just showing up out of nowhere after all this time."

I offer her a closed-lipped smile. "It's just not what I pictured."

Nellie sucks in a breath when I use her words from before, but she was right. Sometimes the hardest part about change isn't even that it's happening. It's not the way your life is altered or the consequences that may come. It's the fact that you've grown so accustomed to something being one way that when it switches, you're thrown. Caught off guard. Left completely exposed and unbalanced.

Suddenly, her understanding is too much, and when her foot brushes against me, I catch the thread of her jeans between my fingers and don't let go.

I can't

"This is the tough conversation, isn't it?" she whispers. "Telling your family about your dad."

I blow out a breath, the taste of wine coating my tongue. "Yep, especially my mom. He left her out of nowhere, and she crawled her way back, finally happy—over it, even—after all this time. And now I'm just supposed to tell her he's coming around again? How? When? Somewhere between the roast turkey and the gingerbread cookies?"

She pauses, her focus on the thread between my fingers. "Is he?" she asks softly. "Coming around?"

"I don't know." I watch as my hand drops the string and settles against her ankle—warm, grounding.

Maybe Nellie should flinch. Freeze. Fidget in her spot until my palm slips off. But she doesn't.

"He wants to. He's said that much. So, I guess it's up to me."

Her gaze is steady—strong. "And what do *you* want?"

"Answers," I admit too quickly. "A conversation. Maybe even a second chance for both of us." I exhale, brushing my thumb across her skin without even realizing it. Goosebumps spread across her ankle, and *dammit*—I feel them everywhere. "Is that shitty?" I ask, suddenly needing her answer.

She shakes her head, inching closer to me. Neither of us acknowledges the shift that's occurring between us. Or the fact that we're sharing a moment, not just secrets. "I don't think so."

My jaw tightens with the truth I'm most afraid to admit to my family. It's all a lot—too much, too fast—but in the best possible way. Fueled by the wine and our circumstances. I lean my forearm on my knee, needing to close more of the gap between us.

"I think if I'm honest, I wished for this. Hoped for it? Damn... maybe even dreamt it would happen. But I think I'm scared that gaining him will cause me to lose the rest of them, you know? And what if he hasn't changed? Or if he has, and it's not enough. What if nothing comes of it?"

Her head drops as she pulls her bottom lip between her teeth. "I get that."

Before I can stop myself, everything I wanted to say before about her story comes to the forefront of my mind. I slide my first finger under her chin and lift. "You talk about your art like it's gone," I say when her eyes finally meet mine. "Like nothing's come of it. But I saw your face light up." I tighten my jaw. "It doesn't seem gone."

Her chest rises, her lips parting, and my hand drops to her shoulder until it trails down to her wrist. She doesn't pull away, and I don't stop myself. I grip the fabric of her sleeve—her damn angel wing—and tug her forward. Our breaths meet, our mouths almost touching. Time seems to stop—or fly or cease to exist—the only reality being that our little adventure, this damn nor 'easter, somehow landed us here.

"I'm gonna kiss you now, Noelle Joy," I admit to her, my voice lower than it's been. "Is that okay?"

Her nod is slow but with intention, not hesitation. "Ye—"

Suddenly, the door bangs open, and I whip around.

"What the—hey! What are you two doing in here?" The fluorescent light from the hallway streams into the dimly lit room, illuminating the round body of a cleaner.

I feel Nellie pull away without even seeing it, her presence gone, her lips no longer inches away.

I clear my throat, turning back to find her scrambling to put on her boots and grab the wine, and I can't help but smile.

"Oh, uh..." she starts to explain.

"Listen, man," I say, looking over my shoulder.

The balding man with an unkept beard sighs, closing the door enough to cover us from those in the hallway and stopping us in our tracks. "Look," he says. "Get out now and leave what's left in those bottles, and I won't call security."

I spin back around to find Nellie wide-eyed and snort out a laugh that I can't stop from escaping. I stand without hesitation, grabbing her hand on the way and pulling her with me. We both search for our bags, clumsy and frantic like kids caught under bleachers. The whole time, the cleaner waits, eyes rolled toward the ceiling.

Once our backpacks are on and her gift bags are slung over the handle of her carry-on, we dart for the exit. We push past the man and through the door. I look over at Nellie, whose face is covered with excitement as she pushes past a group of women standing outside of the bathrooms.

We rush down the hall toward another adventure, the wine—and the taste of what almost happened—still on our lips.

7

Nellie

Leaning our backs against the floor-to-ceiling length windows, Brett and I struggle to catch our breaths. Between the running and the laughing and the wine-induced haze, there was barely room for breathing on the stretch back toward the main gates.

"Do you think he's gonna drink it and go back to work, or is that it? He's calling it, and staying in the closet," Brett pants.

I stand up straight, dropping my gift bags by my feet as I fight my dry mouth. "I think that might be it," I laugh. "Ralph didn't seem too motivated to mop floors."

He turns his head toward me, eyebrow cocked. "Ralph?"

I shrug, pushing off the window. "He was wearing a nametag," I say casually, as if everyone in our situation would have noticed the pin's unique shade of blue.

Brett tips his chin up, his mouth forming an O-shape that reminds me of exactly what the cleaner interrupted. Suddenly, any previous tipsyness passes, and my cotton-mouth has less to do with dehydration and more to do with our almost-kiss.

"I guess we're, uh, trendsetters," I joke, trying to brush off the moment.

He drops his palms onto his hips and turns to me. He hovers above me like he always has, but now it's more alluring.

More enticing.

Just... *more.*

"Literally always. Have you met me?" He drags his hand down the front of his sweater playfully, but I follow it like a treasure map.

My eyes trail back up his chest to his face, and when they return to his, they're darker, hooded. I try to respond—to say anything but *ask me again*—but my words get lodged in my throat.

Brett takes a step toward me, threading a strand of my hair in his hand and letting it slip through his fingers. "Nellie, I—"

"Attention all Golden City travelers." A cheerful sing-song voice chirps over the airport speakers, cutting him off. "This is another friendly reminder that all flights will be delayed until morning due to inclement weather. We will remain grounded as the snow continues to come down heavily. We'll update departure boards as soon as that information is available. Thank you and Merry Christmas Eve eve!"

Brett and I both smile weakly before he glances over his shoulder at the snow. "It really is coming down, isn't it?"

We turn toward the windows, our arms brushing against each other as we watch swirls of white swallow the tarmac. "From every direction," I say in awe.

I see him peer over at me from the corner of my eye, but even more... I feel it. Everything between us seems bigger now, even just standing here—heavier. Our proximity, my tone, his eye contact. Like our near-kiss experience is still with us—a stark shadow casting a tint over everything.

The snow falls in sheets, whipping sideways past the glass. Icicles cling to what can be seen of the immobilized planes outside, feet of snow piled around the wheels. The world is a blur, the horizon tilted, driven sideways by the horizontal winds. Soft orbs of light shine through the picture, almost as if glitter is catching what little sun hides behind the clouds. I realize they are the lights on the apron being consumed by the flurries when Brett interrupts our silence.

"Hey." He places his hands on the window and leans in as snow whirls past in every direction. "It almost looks like we're in a..."

"Snow globe," we say simultaneously.

Brett stands back up and shoves his hands into his pockets. "Yeah," he says. "Exactly."

I smile up at him as long as I can until I'm afraid I might actually wrap my arms around his neck. After those lengthy few seconds, I force my attention back to the whirring puffs of white.

"Hey, for what it's worth..." I start. Brett turns to me, but I keep my eyes fixed on the window as I continue. "I think you're doing the right thing talking to your dad."

He sucks in a breath and turns away again. The silence returns, but only briefly. "I just hope my family thinks so."

"They will," I shoot back. I answer with strength—confidence. Like I know it's true. Like I need it to be. "They might not at first. They might need time or space, but they'll come around. Because you matter to them. And this matters to you."

When I risk looking back at him, I find him staring at his reflection in the window like it might reveal his fate. "The same goes for you."

My brow creases as I try to keep up.

"I'm sure your town just doesn't understand," he says. "They're used to things being only one way. That's how it's always been—it's all they know. But it's okay to be the first to change course or try something new. Honestly? It's brave." He turns his head. "We both are, I guess."

My chest grows tight, a lump forming in my throat that I can barely swallow down. I don't look over because I'm afraid that if I do, the tears building behind my eyes will spill over.

"And the art will come," he continues, softer now. "It might not feel like it, but it's always been there. Deep down, you still want it despite the betrayal you feel now. And someday when you least expect it, it'll come back. And only then will you realize how much you've missed it."

A wave of something close to hope—or peace or understanding—washes over me, but probably not in how Brett intended. Do I wish I'd found my footing in the art world by now? Of course I do. It's my dream—my passion. And it's the *real* reason I'm here. But that doesn't mean I have regrets about leaving Frostpine Falls.

The world is too big to feel so stuck in one place. To stay somewhere surrounded by people you've already met who know your history, your mom, and your goddamn shoe size. And that—*this*—is why I left. For the possibility of crossing paths with people I never would have met otherwise. For the opportunity to share a fleeting moment with a stranger in a real-life snow globe, where, despite our differences, he seems to just... get it.

I revel in this feeling, not stopping myself when I feel the urge to reach out and link my pinky with his. "Like your dad," I say, giving his finger a gentle squeeze.

Brett peers down at me, his eyes distant. "Maybe," he says.

I smile softly just before a yawn escapes my lips. I drop his pinky, my hand flying to my mouth to cover it. "Oh my God, not again. I'm so sorry," I apologize.

"Don't be." He rolls his shoulders back and stands taller. "It's getting late."

I shake my head. "It's the wine."

Brett chuckles. "You sure it isn't our wild adventure?"

I run my hand through my hair and laugh. "That too."

Brett looks around, spinning in a slow circle to take in our surroundings for the first time since we stopped. He pauses when he faces an area dripping with luxury and ambiance, a man standing in front like some sort of security. "Oh, shit," he blurts, his back still to me.

"What?" I ask, searching for the source of his excitement.

"I can't believe I forgot about that."

I step up onto my tiptoes and attempt to look around him. "Will you tell me what's going on?"

He looks back, a giddy smile on his beautiful face, the Brett I've come to know returning. Once again, he grabs my wrist. "Come with me."

And just like before, I do, sliding my palm effortlessly into his.

"You mean to tell me you've had access to this place this entire time?" My eyes wander the VIP lounge that Brett somehow forgot existed, the empty chairs and warm elegance an extreme contrast to what's on the other side of the door.

"I've never needed it," he snaps back. "I go home like twice a year, and don't really make a habit out of spending extra time hanging around the airport."

A server passes as we walk the length of the dimly lit room, a tray of complimentary champagne in his hand. I'm tempted to take one—just to say I did—but I simply gawk at him instead. "Then why do you have the membership?" I question, my voice hushed. Thanks to the man at the door, who *was* in fact security, I know this is not your typical first-class freebie. There was a card involved. And photo ID.

Brett stops mid-stride and turns to me. "Come on." He gestures to himself with high brows. "Do you know who you're adventuring with?"

I tilt my head down and narrow my gaze, waiting for his answer.

"I'm a star, Nellie—important. I make the big bucks, remember?"

I cross my arms over my chest. If he would have answered this way a few hours ago, I would have rolled my eyes and walked away. But by now, I know Brett better than I could have imagined was possible in such a short time.

He keeps his face serious for another beat before letting his shoulders fall. "Okay, okay," he finally surrenders. "My grandma bought it for me last Christmas." I nod, actually believing him this time, and he shrugs innocently. "At least now I can tell her I used it."

"Excuse me, sir... ma'am..." A well-dressed woman in a navy blue pantsuit approaches us as he finishes his sentence. "Welcome. I wanted to let you know that the bar is open, there is a full menu available for dining 24/7, and one of our Sleep Suites has just been reset if you're interested."

"Sleep Suite?" I accidentally say aloud.

Brett smirks when the woman with the slicked-back low bun gives me her attention. "A small, private room for napping or resting."

I smile politely rather than explain to her that I assumed as much, I'm just still completely thrown by the lounge's existence, Brett, and this entire freaking day.

"Thank you," he says, placing his hand on my lower back and guiding me away. When we reach a crossroads—either to the food and drinks or the infamous suites, he stops. "Are you hungry?" he asks.

The question hangs in the air—mixing with that shadow of our fleeting supply closet moment—but his eyes betray him, filling with an anticipation that only occurs when your fate is in question. It's as if he's tossed a coin, and what comes out of my mouth will determine which side it lands on. One word in either direction that has the potential to change our entire trajectory.

With that in mind, my honest response rolls off my tongue before I can second-guess it. "No," I say faintly. "Just... tired."

Brett's throat moves up and down, his jaw tight, until his dimple-framed smile returns. "Well, alright then," he says, his voice cracking halfway through. "Let's find that suite."

We walk next to each other down the short hallway that the employee pointed to. Each step is like a mile until we make it to the only one of the four doors where the privacy indicator above the knob flashes green. "I guess this is it," Brett says, a hum of anticipation between us.

"I guess so," I say back.

He searches my eyes, maybe for acknowledgement about what this could mean—or to give me a chance to back out. Neither of us has come right out and said that entering this shoebox-sized room after we almost kissed might result in something happening. But we haven't had to. The lingering eye contact, the deep conversation, the way his fingers burned through my shirt when they grazed my lower back—it's all there. Written out in flashing red lights like the flight cancellations that started all this.

With that, Brett reaches around me and pushes the door open. I walk in with him and my carry-on at my heels, taking in our new surroundings. The room is even smaller than I thought—literally a double bed with a small shelf on the wall for personal items and an outlet to charge your devices while you nap.

For a second, my body relaxes as I imagine finally laying it down somewhere that's not a cement floor or surrounded by people. But then I look over my shoulder to find Brett so close my nose nearly brushes cashmere, and my senses are heightened all over again.

"Wow, this is..."

"Nice," he says hesitantly.

"I was going to say tiny," I admit.

He heaves a sigh of relief, the warm air buzzing past me. "So small."

He steps forward so we're next to each other, and I drop my backpack on the bed. "You sleep," he says, hiking his up higher on his shoulders. "There's film I can watch on my phone in the lounge."

A disappointment I wasn't expecting swirls in my stomach. I'd like to blame it on the tension between us and the fact that his leaving means nothing would come from that now. But the reality is, we've been with each other for hours, and still, I'm not sick of it. I really like being near him. And I'm not ready to watch him walk out of this hole-in-the-wall only to fall asleep and wake up with less hours left together before we go our separate ways.

"You can stay," I say eagerly as he reaches for the doorknob. Brett pauses in his tracks before spinning back toward me. "Do you have headphones?"

He nods.

"Well, you can watch your film in here then. It's not fair if you don't get to lie down too."

Brett smiles. There's no fooling either of us—we both know the couches and chairs in the lounge are of premium quality and probably feel like sitting on clouds. "I don't want to take up too much room," he says, offering me another out.

I wave him off, moving my backpack to the foot of space between the wall and the edge of the bed. "It's fine, really."

Leaving no more room for arguments—which I'm telling myself is because I'm kind and generous and not because I'm hungry and needy for something that's most definitely not on the dining menu—I slide onto the far side of the mattress and lay my head on the pillow.

"Okay then," Brett chuckles and lets his backpack slide off of his shoulders and onto the open side of the bed. He unzips the small pocket and digs around briefly before blowing out a breath.

"What?" I ask, sitting up on my elbows.

"I think I forgot my headphones."

"Oh," I say, my voice depleted.

"It's okay, I'll just—"

"Use mine," I offer too quickly. *Shit, for being a so-called wolf, I sure know how to beg.*

"Are you sure?"

"Yeah, it's no problem." Sitting up fully, I point to my bag on the floor. "First pocket."

I lay back down as Brett grabs my backpack, contemplating if this is a get under the sheets or stay on top of the blanket situation. He kneels, unzips it, and begins rummaging through. I listen to the sounds of his digging bounce off the walls, trying to slow my mind from the open possibilities that hang in the room.

Then, suddenly, the shuffling stops.

8

Brett

"Holy shit," I say, my voice coming out breathless.

Nellie springs up, her eyes doubling in size when they land on the sketchbook in my hands. She jumps to her knees, grabbing at it. "What are you doing?"

"You said I could get your headphones, and—"

"Does this look like a pair of headphones to you?" she rips the book from my hands, the pages dipping underneath my grasp.

I study her expression, angry and taken aback. "It was in the pocket," I explain, borderline confused.

"I meant the *first* pocket," she argues uncomfortably.

I point to the backpack. "That is the first pocket."

"I mean the first from the fron—" She heaves a deep breath, her body stiff. "Forget it."

My stomach sinks as this whole moment takes a turn, and my gaze falls back to the black and white drawing in her hands. When she notices, she pulls the pages close to her chest, and my puzzled eyes lock with hers. "Nellie, I didn't know you made art like *that*."

"I don't." She closes her eyes tightly, steadying herself. "I don't any-more," she clarifies, her tone still laced with anger.

"You clearly do," I argue. "And it's fucking good."

Her cheeks flush instantly, her face still dripping with frustration. I don't look away despite the heat behind her stare. "Can we just drop it?" she asks harshly.

I shake my head, answering honestly. "I don't think so."

Her face softens briefly, but her hands are still hugged against her. "Brett..."

"Nellie..." I dare to reach up and tuck a loose strand of hair behind her ear. Her jaw tightens, but her eyes relax slightly.

She and I have been in such close proximity since we met that the size of this room didn't even register as anything but normal.

Until now.

I almost kissed her. Shit, I asked, and she said yes. And ever since we were interrupted, the only thing I can think about is what her lips would feel like pressed to mine. Now, with a new form of tension entering the space—seeing what she's capable of and how hesitant she is to share it—I only want her more. And that makes my skin buzz so close to hers.

"You're incredible," I say in double-meaning, desperate to move past this complete one-eighty. She swallows hard, masking her heavy breathing as rage, but her exposed chest betrays her, turning the most delicious shade of pink.

Grateful that it's small, I sit down on the mattress and cautiously reach for her hand. She's reluctant at first, but when I don't cower, she lets me take it in mine. Her gaze falls to where my fingers hang from hers as I gently tug her down. When she lands hesitantly next to me, I prop one knee on the bed, turning toward her. "You have to do this, Nellie."

She looks over her opposite shoulder, avoiding my gaze, but I don't give up that easily. Taking her chin between my thumb and forefinger, I guide her back to me. She looks everywhere but my eyes until I find them with my own.

"Like *really* do this," I continue. Nellie's breath stays heavy, but slowly, the intensity in her expression starts to soften. "And not in the pockets of time that you have here and there or if someone just so happens to give you a chance. Between your talent and how obvious it is that you love it... this is *it* for you."

"I don't think that's true," she counters.

"It is." I pull the sketchbook away from her slowly. She tightens her grip, but then, her resistance wavers until she lets it fall to her lap. "This," I say, pointing to the black and white drawing. "This is your *less than one percent.*"

Nellie scrunches up her adorably freckled nose before remembering she's supposed to be upset. "My what?"

I huff out a laugh, looking back down at the fine lines and light shading that morph together to form the face of man. "Do you know what the chances were of me making it into the NHL?" I ask.

She fights the way the corners of her lips attempt to curl and raises a brow instead. "I'm gonna take a stab in the dark and say less than one percent?"

I nudge her gently and nod. "But here I am. It would have been easy to quit before I even got started, chalking every failure and setback up to the idea that most people don't make it. But the other side of that is... some people do."

She grins—barely, but it's there—and I knock my elbow into hers. I know I should speak—prove my point and tell her all the reasons she can't give this up. But I lose my words in the green of her eyes and the way she doesn't fully pull her arm away.

She clears her throat subtly, and I blink hard, loosening the grip she has on me. "You're gonna do it, Nellie," I say instead.

Her gaze drops to my lips for the briefest of seconds before it bounces back to mine. She shakes her head. "No, I probably won't. But either way, it got me out of Frostpine Falls. I don't think I would have had the courage to leave if I didn't have that ulterior motive."

"What? No," I throw back more harshly than I mean to. I force a breathy laugh and inhale deeply, calming the foreign frustration that begins building in my gut. "Look at this." I knock the sketchbook with my knuckle. "This is fucking art, Nell. And I bet if I flipped through those pages there'd be a dozen more just as good."

She frames the page with her pointer finger, running it along the crisp white edges as her hard exterior falters more. "I don't know about that," she answers softly.

I suck in a deep breath, steadying myself again. "I'm sure they are."

Nellie swallows hard and shrugs. "Well, it doesn't matter."

"But it does," I snap, shifting so I'm facing her head on. That unnecessary irritation resurfaces, and I'm not sure who's more thrown from the role-reversal, her or me. *She's* the one who's supposed to be upset, and I'm supposed to be the one pulling *her* from the trenches.

She squints, taken aback, her expression dripping with the perfect mix of confusion and hurt. She unfolds the cover and slams it shut. "It doesn't, Brett."

My name slipping from her lips hits me in the same place that roughness attempts to escape. It doesn't settle it, though. Instead, it changes it—shifts it into something less trying, more primal. I rub my eyebrow with my thumb, begging my thoughts to sort themselves out before I speak again.

"It should," I argue calmly.

Nellie scoffs, and that deep burn inside of me bubbles to the top. "No offense, but you barely know *me*, let alone my art. Why do you even care?"

I boil over, my real reasoning—my honest answer—flying up from that dark place. A truth I didn't realize until this exact moment, threatening to pour out. The one that's been eating at me since I laid eyes on Nellie's dream. Since I got that first letter from my dad weeks ago. The one I shoved so far down I almost forgot it existed.

But before I can stop myself, it floods from my chest.

"Because *I* need it to matter. *I* need this to happen for you. Because the chances of a kid like me—whose dad didn't even want him—making it to the NHL is literally one in a million. Less than one percent, Nellie. And you know what I thought the odds of him coming back were? Even less. So, yeah, I need you to try. And dammit, *I* need to see it all work out because what are the odds that it happens again? I need to know it wasn't a fluke. I need to know that little kid—with a dream and a stick in his hands but no fucking father—making it to the Flames wasn't just luck. That this shit happens. *Miracles* happen. Dreams come true and people come back and the world doesn't fucking burn down when they do."

When I'm finally done, my chest is heaving as my breath shoots out in brief spurts. My jaw grows tight as I try to gauge Nellie's reaction and attempt to piece together some form of explanation or apology that will justify jumping down her throat.

She doesn't know me. Shit, she was right—I don't know her either, despite the fact that it feels like I do. We've been forced together in crammed hallways, tight closets, tiny beds—small spaces with nothing but time on our hands.

Our circumstances deceived me into getting too comfortable. My dread over going back home, the holiday snow globe we're trapped inside of, the wine, the goddamn sleeves she's wearing disguised as angel wings—all of it tricked my brain into spilling confessions I barely even recognize.

But none of it's real.

Not outside of this moment...

Or is it?

Before I can decide, Nellie's lips crash into mine.

At first, I freeze—caught somewhere between heaven and the black hole I briefly fell into—but as soon as she brings her hand to my cheek, all of my senses kick back on. My hand flies into the hair I've wanted to run my fingers through since I held it at the windows as I inhale deeply, soaking up every bit of her being this close. I breathe in the cinnamon that wafts off of her, as the lingering sweetness from the wine seeps through her lips.

Nellie drops her palm to my thigh, and I exhale heavily as she digs the tips of her fingers into the muscle. She sweeps her tongue past my lips, and I meet it with mine—eager to finally let her in. Reaching around her lower back, I yank her closer until our legs—and her sketchbook—are the only barriers between us. I hold her there as she plays with the hair at the nape of my neck, tugging it gently before pulling away.

Once again, I search her expression, praying I don't find a hint of regret in her evergreen eyes. Waiting for her to make the next move, I soak up the tousle in her hair and the pink in her cheeks that *I* put there.

Nellie looks at me, her face full of clarity. She sets the pad of paper next to her and pushes up onto her knees to move toward me. Straddling my lap, she wraps her arms around my shoulders and settles her weight where I'm already hard.

"Nellie, we don't have to do this," I tell her, tucking a stray hair behind her ear.

She looks down at me. "Oh, now I get a say in what I do?" My eyes go wide until she grins. "I kissed *you*, remember?"

"I know, thank God." I smile, leaning in to press my lips to hers once again, more grateful than I realized to see her happy again. But my face grows serious as I pull away. "But that doesn't mean we have to do *this*."

She huffs out a laugh, and I clench my teeth. "What?" I ask, confused by her reaction.

She shakes her head and dips her fingers underneath the neck of my sweater. "Nothing," she says coyly.

My whole body stiffens as I narrow my eyes. "Okay, you can't laugh while we're sitting like *this* and not tell me why. I'm pretty sure that's the law."

She crinkles her nose. "Here? Or in Canada?"

"Both," I say definitively. "It's like a whole world thing. You should probably know that considering you went to college." Attempting not to laugh again, she turns her lips in, but she smiles with her eyes. "Tell me," I say, my tone more stern.

Nellie's lips slowly unfold as she looks at me intensely. She peers down at the drawing now at the corner of the bed, then finds me again. "You just really are one of the good ones." With that, she leans back in, and I can't help it... I kiss her hard and nibble gently on her lip.

She whimpers into my mouth as her grip grows tighter around my neck and she pushes her chest further into mine. "I want this," she whispers when I reluctantly let go.

"Are you sure?" I ask as she presses her mouth to my neck.

"Honestly," she pants. "This is the thing I'm *most* sure of right now."

With those words as permission, I wrap my arm around her waist and lift until I can slide back onto the pillows. I lower her down, and she falls forward, bracing herself on either side of my head. I reach for her ass, pinning her to my cock desperate for friction, and Nellie moans as she nips at my ear.

She reaches for the hem of my sweater, and I sit up, giving her the full access she needs to strip it off. Her eyes trail my arms and chest before dipping down to the V by my jeans, and when they return to mine, they're heated and hungry.

She drops her hands to the bottom of her shirt and rips it over her head, her top and wings both falling to the floor. I let my gaze drop to her chest—full, perfect—straining against the sheer white lace that's left. Nellie slips her hands behind her back and, seconds later, the bra falls in between us. I reach out, holding her in my hands, brushing my thumbs across her peaked, aching nipples.

"You're not a wolf, Nellie Joy," I say as she slides down the front of me. My voice grows husky when she reaches for the button at my waist. "You're a goddamn angel."

She offers me a shy smile as she unzips my pants. I growl as she tugs at my belt loops, then lift my lower half so she can slide my jeans down. When they reach my ankles, I sit up, kicking them off. Nellie stands in the small space between the wall and the foot of the bed—right next to the backpack I once searched that started all this.

I dip my fingers into the front of her jeans, tugging her closer. "You're sure?" I ask again, rubbing my thumb along the cool metal of her button.

I peer up to find her already looking at me—waiting for my eyes to meet hers. "You don't have to keep asking," she says when they finally do.

I let my head fall forward as I breathe out. "I just... I didn't plan for this to happen."

"You mean you didn't plan to be burned by your own coffee, survive off of vending machine snacks and wine all night, be serenaded by French exchange students, caught by an airport employee, and then seduce me in the world's smallest room after I snap on you about my art?"

I stare up at her, eyebrows high. "Yeah, pretty much."

"I know." She works around my fingers, undoing the button herself. "And that's why you're so... so *good.*" The zip of her jeans bounces off the walls around us, but I can't take my eyes off of her face, steady and unwavering. "And that's why these things you're afraid can't happen twice are both happening to you."

Nellie wiggles her hips back and forth until both her jeans and her underwear fall right to the floor. But what's most captivating isn't the sight in front of me. It's the words pouring from her lips that have my attention.

"I've known you for half a day, and I can already tell that you're warm and honest and that you think about others more than yourself. It's why this life-altering thing is happening to *you*, yet you're most worried about your family's reactions." I search her face as she continues, my chest filling as she strips me bare. "I mean, your dad left when you were so young, and I haven't heard a word about what that did to *you*."

I stare at the carpet beneath her feet.

The day he left, my dad left a father-sized hole in my life—and my heart. Nothing was the same. Even when Tom came around, that space wasn't filled, not completely. I think I just learned to live with it. It's like playing a man short on the penalty kill. At first, the ice feels too big—too empty. But as the seconds pass, you adjust. You fill gaps, cover holes, and eventually, you find a new rhythm with what you have left.

I'm always the funny one—the comedic relief. I'm goofy and loveable and over the top, but most see me as good for a laugh, not just *good*. I talk too much and stand too close and, honestly, I'm a lot to take in. But I always figured being *too much* just meant I was never *too little*. That at least that meant I was *enough*. Enough for my mom, my family, my team—enough to make people stay.

"I'm good?" I question, not realizing that I've said it out loud.

Nellie nods. "Like human sunshine."

"And adorable..." I press playfully.

She smiles. "Like a puppy."

I sigh, but somehow my chest feels full. "I'm good," I whisper to myself.

"It's why I kissed you first, straddled your lap, and am standing naked in front of you, yet you keep asking if I'm sure I want this." Her eyebrows lift as the corners of her lips curve upward. Only then do I let my focus fall to the artwork in front of me, my hands sliding down the curve of her waist. "And so... yes, I'm sure," she continues. She crawls back on top of me again. "Now, would you please stop being so polite?"

A guttural sound rips from my throat as I wrap her up and flip us both over. Nellie throws her legs around my waist and her arms around my neck as I carry her back to the top of the bed. Laying her down, I back off just enough to take her in again.

I plant a kiss on her lips, then at the soft spot behind her ear. Moving down her neck, I nip and suck my way to her chest until I finally reach her swollen nipples. I roll my tongue over the peaks as Nellie arches her back. She shifts beneath me, kneading her heels into the mattress, searching for more.

"Touch me, Brett," she begs, grabbing hold of my wrist by her side.

I suck in a breath, walking my hand between her legs. Dragging my fingers down her inner thigh, I prepare myself for what I know will be true. Touching her—being *inside* her—is going to ruin me in the best possible way.

There's something about Noelle Joy Winters that will separate every sexual experience I *have* ever had and *will* ever have into *before* her and *after* her. Maybe it's this whole thing—the airport adventure I never expected, bonding with her after being trapped together and sharing some of our deepest secrets.

Or maybe it's just her—us. As if another less-than-one-percent moment has happened without me even realizing it.

Somehow in the middle of an airport, with the world covered in white, I found someone I wasn't even looking for.

9
Nellie

"Touch me, Brett," I beg, grabbing a hold of his wrist by my side.

Brett sucks in a breath, walking his hand between my legs. He drags his fingers down my inner thigh, and I revel in the anticipation of finally exploring each other.

It seems like we've been intimate all day—sharing tight spaces and quiet secrets. But all that's done is make me want him physically. Any girl would be attracted to the six-foot-something brick-house, hockey legend even without him opening his mouth. But then he hits you with his sweet heart and stupid humor, and who wouldn't be hooked? Add in that he's let me in on his fears and turmoil—shared the one thing he's having the hardest time dealing with—and it's as if he stripped naked right in front of me way before now.

After what feels like an eternity, Brett finally dips his hand between my thighs, my legs already quivering as he palms my pussy that's been waiting for this—for him. His head lulls back as he slides two fingers up my center and groans. "My God, Nellie," is all he says before he slides both of them into me.

I cry out, and Brett brings the pointer on his opposite hand to my lips, reminding me that this box that we're in isn't exactly secluded. I bite down on the bottom one as he glides in and out of me, his cock rock hard against my thigh.

I close my eyes as he works his fingers, sweeping his thumb past my clit. I swirl my hips, grinding against his touch, not realizing he's dropped to his knees in the meantime. When his fingers slide from my pussy clenched around them, my head snaps forward. I part my lips to argue—beg him to keep going—until his tongue hits my skin.

"Holy shit," I whimper as he sweeps it up my middle.

My hand flies to his hair, which I didn't realize was so thick and full until my fingers were threaded into it, and I hold on to the locks like a lifeline. He growls as I pull on it, his face still buried between my thighs, his mouth still licking and sucking in all the right places.

"A fucking angel," he breathes into me, the warm air only intensifying the sensation.

I let my head sink back into the pillow, my eyelids falling shut once again. Images of our day together flash in my mind like an edit of the short time that we've known each other. They mix with reality, the two ripping through my head like the snow is outside. A flash of his smile, then a tease of him shirtless. Us laughing in the gift shop, then a hum against my clit. Sitting on the supply closet floor, airing out secrets—sharing, connecting—then he shoves his fingers back inside.

It all hits me when a memory of him staring at my art, telling me to go for my dream—with passion in his eyes and gravity in his tone—blends with the current grip he has on my thigh. Brett had me the second he brushed off my assault on his jacket. The minute he latched on to me so I didn't feel so alone. The moment he spun this whole thing into our very own adventure.

He undressed me with his humor, seduced me with his innocence, satisfied me by baring his soul—and listening to me bare mine. This, right now, with his hands and his mouth pushing me closer and closer to the edge, is a bonus. Brett Burns etched himself into my soul hours ago and then again just now when he fought off my bitterness. By being here.

By being *him*.

"Oh my God," I cry, my back lifting off the mattress.

Brett continues his relentless pursuit until my body goes weak and the only parts of him still on me are the marks he dug into my leg when he white-knuckled his hold.

"Come here," I pant, reaching for him.

He stands first, slipping out of his tight black briefs, springing to life as he reaches for his jeans' pocket. When he stands, wrapper in hand, he stills for a moment, holding my gaze with his jaw tight and his fist wrapped around his cock, almost as if he's giving me one last chance to back out.

"Come here," I repeat, my voice steady and strong.

Brett obeys, slinking up my legs until he hovers over me, his palms on either side of my shoulders. "You have no idea how bad I want you right now," he admits, dipping down to kiss up my throat.

"Then have me," I say, opening both my neck and legs up to him.

He looks at me—*really* looks at me—the same way he always seems to do when he's listening. "I know you probably don't believe this..." He hangs his head between his arms. I run my hand through his hair until he finds me again. "But I don't do this as much as you might think."

"I thought the Burns' Effect was strong," I quip, smiling slyly.

Brett grins, huffing out a laugh. "Oh, it is." His face grows more serious before he continues. "But so is... I'm..."

"You're what?"

He bends down and softly presses his lips to mine. "Well, I'm like a puppy, remember?"

His words wash over me, funny at first as we both smile, but then they really sink in. I thought initially that he was hoping I wouldn't do something that I might regret later. But now I realize that was only half of it. The other part wasn't reassurance—it was a plea. A warning.

"We don't have to do this," I tell him, reminding him of what he has continuously said to me.

He thinks about it briefly, his eyes wandering mine until he shakes his head, running his thumb down my cheek. "I don't think it would change anything."

I swallow his admittance, telling him that I'm right there with him in the only way I can manage. My mind tells me this is crazy. We met hours ago and had it not been for this nor 'easter—this stupid cancellation—then we wouldn't even know each other. But as he kisses me back, his body sinking into mine, I realize... that's the point.

We are the one in a million. The miracle. The less-than-one-percent. The chance that two strangers from this big city smash into each other beneath the same departure board and just so happen to end up here? Slim to none.

Yet, here we are.

If Brett was looking for a hat trick, he found it. I don't need to make it in the art world—*we* are his proof that these things do happen.

Our tongues intertwine, rolling over each other, eager and deliberate. I wrap my legs around Brett's back, pushing him closer, the base of him lining up perfectly with where I need him most. He groans into me, then sits back on his heels just long enough to slide the condom on. I watch as it rolls down the length of him, waiting—searching—for an ounce of hesitation.

But it doesn't come.

When he's finished, Brett leans down, sliding his arm under my back. I squeal when he flips us both again, and he shushes me, his boyish smile on full display.

His face hardens as I prop myself up on my knees, taking his cock into my hand. It's big and beautiful—unexpectedly so—just like him, and my pussy aches at the sight of it. I line him up with my center, both of us smothering our cries as I lower myself down. Brett's palms fly to my thighs, his chin lifting as his head presses into the pillow. I sink slowly, taking him just a few inches at a time, my knees digging into his ribs as I brace myself on either side of them.

"Fuck, Nellie," he says once my ass is flush against him.

I shift slowly as he grabs the back of my neck and pulls me forward. The angle forces him higher, and my walls clench around him. "You're so deep," I admit.

Brett kisses me, dragging his hand down the center of my back, and as if that one touch was all I needed, I sit up again and begin rocking back and forth. He holds my hips as I grind against him, my body already close. I pick up speed, our breathing heavy. That sound becomes the only one in the room as I slide on and off him, his hips bucking up to meet me. When he rolls my nipples between his fingers, my pussy starts to quiver.

"Oh my God," I whisper, partially because of our surroundings, but mostly because it feels so good I can barely speak.

I come undone as Brett holds me at my hips, steadying them as he pounds into me. When I fall onto his chest, he grabs my ass, massaging it as he nuzzles himself into my hair. I take a moment to catch my breath, but as I do, he brings his mouth to my ear. "You're gonna come again for me, Angel," he says, his tone dark.

I push off of him and look into his eyes. They're still his—sweet, kind, innocent—but there's a depth to them I haven't seen yet. A strength—a power—that I lose myself in.

That gives me power too.

I nod, lifting myself off of him. Brett narrows his eyes, curious but trusting. When I spin around, straddling his lap in the opposite direction, he sucks in a breath. "Oh, shit," he gasps as I sit back down. I look back at him, and he reaches forward, brushing my hair over my shoulder. "Goddamn, Nellie," he says, tugging on it gently. "You're perfect."

"I'm not," I argue.

"You are." He sits forward, taking my chin in his hands. "Best Christmas ever."

I laugh, but he swallows it, kissing me with a need that wasn't there before. He drops his hand to my chest, massaging and tugging until he stops to press on the center of my back, pushing me forward.

I brace myself on his shins as I begin shifting back and forth, his cock filling me even more in this position. My lips part, my head hanging between my arms, as Brett thrusts underneath me, meeting me halfway. We move together in perfect harmony—not awkward or messy like it *can* be as strangers—but naturally, like we've always been there. Exactly as it's been from the start.

When I lean back, moving my hands from his shins to either side of his hips, Brett blows a heavy breath through his lips. "Fuck," he moans.

His massive leg muscles tighten as he somehow grows harder inside me. "God, Angel, don't stop."

I don't—I can't—not teetering this close to the edge. I grind faster, both of us panting as Brett slides his hands on top of mine, interlocking our fingers. I grip him back, the gesture almost too much to take. We hold on to each other—anchoring ourselves to one another.

Then, we free fall together.

10

Brett

I stir awake, my arm flying from above my head to the side of my body laying naked underneath the blanket. It takes me a second—and a quick glance around the too-small room—to remember where I am.

And who I'm with.

I roll my head to the side, the warmth of her body wedged against mine, her hair cascading down my chest as she sleeps. I freeze, too nervous that if I move even an inch, she'll wake up and leave. Or worse—she'll realize this was a mistake after all.

I listen to her slow, sleepy breaths, watching as her shoulder rises and falls with each one. It hits me that I have no idea how long we've been here. It could have been twenty minutes or three hours. It could be morning or we could have missed our flights completely and slept right through the next day.

I'm caught between wanting to check the time and not caring enough to wake her. Fortunately—or not—a soft set of bells rings out from a speaker in the ceiling I didn't know existed and decides our fate for me.

"Wake up call," an airy voice speaks over the alarm. "Your time in the Sleep Suite will come to an end in ten minutes."

The bells sound again, followed by the same cheerful yet robotic voice repeating the message. By the time it goes off for the third time, Nellie stirs beside me.

"What time is it?" she questions, her voice still half-asleep.

I slip my arm out from under her reluctantly and bend it just enough to see my wrist. "Like three in the morning."

"What the hell?" She sits up, pulling the blanket with her to cover her chest.

"I think there's a time limit on these things," I say, swirling my finger in a circle, pointing to the room.

Nellie nods, rubbing sleep from her eyes as I stare at her back, memorizing the way her hair falls in waves and her freckles faintly mark her skin. She stills, facing forward, both of us silent.

When she glances back at me, the image of her doing the same just hours ago haunts me in the best possible way. Every look, every sound, every touch floods my senses all over again. With only that on my mind, I extend my arm and brush my knuckles against her back.

Nellie twists further toward me, and I hold my breath. She pulls her bottom lip between her teeth and holds my gaze. After a stillness that feels like an eternity, her mouth forms a smile, then the bells chime again.

We both laugh lazily as I run my hand through her hair. She runs her hands through her own, tucking it behind her ears. "I guess they're kicking us out."

"Do you think if we leave and come back in our time resets?" I ask.

Nellie grins and shakes her head. "Probably not."

I sigh, bracing my weight on my hands and sliding up. "Worth a shot."

She looks away, her eyes wandering the room. I don't realize what she's doing until she tugs the blanket tighter around her chest.

"Oh, here, let me give you a minute." I get up, careful not to flash her how excited I was to wake up beside her, and find my briefs. Yanking them on, I finally stand, find my jeans, and slip inside of them before turning to face her. "I'm gonna go check out the food situation," I say, reaching for my sweater. I pull it over my head as Nellie tracks every inch of my movement, then I slide my backpack onto my shoulders. "I'll meet you out there?"

The corners of her lips curl as she nods, and it's all I need really—just the slightest of signs that she doesn't regret this whole thing ever happened. That I didn't completely scare her away.

I unlock the door and slip out, resisting the urge to glance back at her once more. I was right. I knew I would be. I'm leaving this suite differently than when I first entered it. Nellie Joy left her mark. Her mind, her body, her words—all a part of me.

At least for now.

"What are you getting?" I peer over the menu the lounge employee dropped at our table to find Nellie wide-eyed.

"I don't know... all of it? Why am I so hungry?"

A breath catches in my throat—all the jokes I'd normally make stuck behind it. For some reason, they won't come out. My usual *Burns' Effect, baby* or *you're welcome* don't slip. Instead, Helen's reminder rings in my ear—*with the right person, being real will be enough.*

"Probably because you've eaten nothing but high fructose corn syrup and red dye number forty for the last ten plus hours."

"Don't forget the alcohol—there was a grape or two thrown in there somewhere."

I laugh, scanning the menu. "Yeah, you're right—practically a fruit salad."

Nellie raises her brows in challenge then offers me a smile. "Do you think the flights are posted yet?"

I shake my head. "I asked when I sat down if they knew anything. They said they still haven't been updated."

She nods, and I swear I see a dip of relief in her shoulders.

"But they think they will be soon," I add, setting my menu on the table and meeting her gaze.

"Oh." She does the same and interlocks her fingers, bruising one thumb over the other. "Well, that's good then."

Is it?

"For sure." I sit up straighter and rest my forearms on the table. "We'll both be headed home soon."

Nellie takes a vested interest in the dessert section—ironic considering our previous statements. I pick mine back up and scan the entrees, my mind anywhere but on the Mahi Mahi.

"So, how long are you staying?"

My head pops up, but she's not looking at me. In fact, half of her face is now covered by the paper. I don't answer right away, getting lost in the way her eyelashes flutter as her eyes dance across the page. I will them to lift—beg her to look at me so I can gauge her thoughts even a little. But they don't.

"At home," she adds, waiting.

"Just a few days," I say cheerfully. Now her lids fly open, and her eyes land on me. "We have a home game on the twenty-eighth."

"Cool," she says nonchalantly.

"How about you?"

"Ten days. Well... nine now, I guess. I come home the day after New Year's."

I scan the drinks. "That's a long visit." I risk a glance at Nellie, but she isn't looking at me. Instead, she's staring tight-jawed, watching the bead of condensation on her water glass slide toward the table.

"So, what now?" she asks through a deep inhale.

My entire body tenses, struck by surprise. I run through our options—we could talk while she's gone and meet up when she returns. Maybe she'd come back early so we could ring in the New Year together? We definitely have options. It's just over a week, and despite that feeling like years after spending every second together, I know *I'll* be counting down the days until she gets back to Golden City.

My lips part to run through my thoughts, but she speaks before I can.

"I guess we could hang here and wait until they update the flights."

I press my lips shut and paint a smile. "Sure," I say. "Whatever you want."

In perfect timing, an employee comes by our table and offers to take our orders. I get a club sandwich, and Nellie opts for a chicken Caesar salad and fries. We sit in silence, waiting for our food to come until the server returns, setting our plates in front of us.

We take our first bites—the first tastes of *proper* food that we've had in hours—and melt into our seats. Those mouthfuls are followed by another and another until we've eaten enough to come up for air. When I do, I look up at Nellie as she brings a fry to her lips.

As if I'm sitting on the bench, I watch her like she's a forward on a breakaway, tracking her movements—the fry is the puck and her mouth is the net. I gape at her, hooked—latched on to each inch of motion.

"What's your plan?" she asks, completely unaware of the trance she just broke. "For telling your parents. Do you have one?"

I wipe my hands on the napkin in my lap. "Not really. I definitely want to talk to my mom first. Maybe wait until after Christmas Day at this point. But I don't want to feel like I'm doing this behind anyone's back, so I guess Tom and Bailey will be next."

"I'm sure they'll understand," she tries to reassure.

I take a bite of my sandwich and buy time, chewing. "I'm not even sure *I* understand, to be honest," I admit. "So, I would get it if they didn't. But I've learned that sometimes people respond to life in the only ways they know how. It's not always right or convenient or how you would react, but it's natural. It's how they survive whatever scares them."

"And you can just forgive him for that?" she asks, her tone defensive.

"No," I answer quickly. "But what does holding it against him do? Who does it hurt? Him, sure—he doesn't get to be a part of his son's life for another twenty years. But the same goes for me. If I decide to let the past dictate the future, then I lose out on that time too."

Nellie listens intently, her fork rolling between her fingers. "Besides," I continue. "In some twisted fate, his leaving was the best thing to ever happen to me."

"What? How?"

I scoff lightly in understanding. It's taken me a long time to get here. "If my dad never left, my mom would have never met Tom, the two of them would have never had Bailey, and I wouldn't have my sister." Her eyes grow glossy. "Not to mention my mom's strength, my resilience..."

"The way you soak up every second."

My chest swells, and I hold my breath. No one has ever said something so plainly to me like that before. I try to find words, but instead, I answer only by sliding my fingers into hers. She doesn't pull away. In fact, her eye contact doesn't even waver.

"I try to."

"I can tell."

I look down at our hands interlocked. "There's always a silver lining."

"Human sunshine," Nellie whispers, giving me a gentle squeeze.

"You're like that too, though. You said it yourself." She tilts her head, curious. "Those years of what you see as failure just gave you the chance to try new things—take on opportunities you wouldn't have had time for otherwise. Do the after-school thing. Meet Ruthie."

"I know. I'm just not sure I see it like you do. If I had the chance to give it all up to get my art back..."

"You would?"

She nods shyly. "I—I think so."

"Well, who says you can't have both?" I brush my thumb along hers.

"I don't know," she sighs. "It's just not the same anymore."

I lick my lips and roll them over each other. "Just... keep an open mind, okay? Maybe it's not so black and white."

She tips her chin down, and peers up at me. "Fine," she agrees, smothering a smile.

"Hey, I have an idea."

Nellie hums and pulls her hand away.

I try to focus on my new plan and ignore the vacancy she leaves behind. "What do you say we go back to the start? Back to your roots?" Nellie wrinkles her brow and narrows her eyes. "Come on, it'll be fun."

She groans teasingly. "Another adventure?"

I cock a brow. "Have I let you down yet?"

11

Nellie

"Still no updates," I say, looking up at the flashing red on the board.

"Perfect," Brett says, glancing over his shoulder. "You stay here. I'll be right back."

"Wait, where..."

My voice fades as he sprints away. I follow him as he walks up to the counter of the coffee stand across the room. The line is still a mile long—it's a wonder they haven't run out of caffeine—but Brett waltzes right up to the register. The women and men alike gawk at him in line. Some stand open-mouthed, some throw him dirty looks. Some even lose their place just to crowd around him.

He flashes a smile, runs his hand through his hair, and then looks nonchalantly back at me. I can't see the clerk behind his broad body, but seconds later, Brett turns around with two giant coffees in hand.

"Son of a bitch," I whisper under my breath.

I stare at the cups as he saunters back and extends one to me. "You did it, didn't you?" I ask, grabbing it.

"Did what?" he asks coyly, blowing a slow breath into the opening in the lid.

My thighs heat at the remembrance of him doing the same between them, and I physically stop myself from inching closer. "The Burns' Effect," I say. "You just used it to get these."

Brett takes a cautious sip and swallows it down. "I plead the Fifth."

I suck my teeth. "Mhmm."

Smirking, he runs his free hand through his hair again, then leans in. "You jealous?" He asks jokingly, tossing it back in casual banter. But the second our eyes meet, the air thickens between us.

"No," I lie, cutting through the tension. "Just confused about what this has to do with your great idea."

He smiles ear to ear, and for a second, I almost nuzzle into him, throw my arms around his neck, and press my lips to his. Instead, I drown the urge in a gulp of coffee.

"What did you say made you really fall in love with art?"

I exhale, my head lolling backward. "Brett, can we just drop this?"

"Just answer the question."

I look at him over my lid and take a sip. Brett's gaze dips down to my lips as I do it, but I pretend not to notice. "Drawing the city," I admit begrudgingly. "People watching."

"People drawing," he corrects. I huff out a laugh as he runs his tongue over his top teeth. "And when's the last time you did that?"

I stare at him, waiting—refusing to answer.

"Come on," he begs.

I sigh, either still too tired or too wrapped up in him to argue. Brett paints a cocky grin, and I narrow my eyes, thinking. "Besides in my Uber here? The verdict's still out on whether that man is a serial killer, by the way."

"Wait, what?" Brett throws back.

I wave him off and exhale another heavy breath. "Besides that, I don't know. A couple of months, maybe. I thought while I was home it might help remind me of why I left in the first place. Not that I'll need a reminder, I'm sure." I get lost for a second, staring at the top of my lid as if the white plastic holds all the comments and questions I'll get back home.

The sarcastic *Oh, how's the big city* and the passive aggressive *Look who isn't too good for little old Frostpine Falls now.* Then, of course, the few who don't squeeze Mom for details at every farmer's market will toss out a *So, what are you doing now that you couldn't do here?* And those who do will hit me with *You know, you didn't need to leave home just to find someone to babysit.*

All of it will bother me. More than it should.

I never left Frostpine Falls because I felt better than. I know that there's good in staying in a place where there are no mysteries, especially in such an uncertain world. And I know that I *could* find something there that may bring me some joy and maybe even use my degree and ability more than I am now.

But Ruthie isn't just someone I'm watching while her dad's away. I'm helping to mold her into the young teenager she's becoming, who is beautiful both inside and out. I teach her, care for her—I'm someone she comes to when she's had a rough day or needs some advice. I'm part of her now, and she's part of me.

"And why did you stop doing it?" Brett asks, drawing me back. "Finding places to sit and sketch?"

I shrug, a heaviness settling into my gut as the truth forms itself on my tongue. "It's just not the same as it used to be. Before, it felt like practice. Like I was bettering myself for when that opportunity hit. Now?" I glance back down at the all-knowing white lid. "Now it feels like... like a waste of time."

"Well, it's not," Brett retorts. "Nothing that occupies space in your mind or causes you this much angst is. But you know what? Even if it was..." He points up, gesturing to the departure board still riddled with red letters and unknown information. "We've got nothing but time to waste."

I freeze, my eyes doubling in size. "Wait, what?" I say, mimicking his earlier response. "What? No."

He nods with excitement.

"No," I repeat.

"Yes."

"Uh uh. Not happening."

Brett flashes me that stupid smile and leans in closer. "Just once," he says, his words hushed and flirtatious.

A heat creeps both into my chest and between my thighs. "So, what am I supposed to do?" I ask, attempting to cover my lust. "Sit on the floor and draw... that guy?" I tip my chin toward a man in an ugly Christmas sweater that I'm almost positive he does *not* think is ugly, with a flashing Christmas bulb necklace that should come with a warning label.

"Well, you definitely could..." Brett says, taking in Mr. Holiday Cheer. He mutters under his breath something about his sweater being dope, then spins back around. "Or... you could draw me."

"You?" Nerves wash over me, my body resisting this whole plan almost as much as my mind.

"Me." He answers confidently. "But not just any version of me. The me that you would have seen if we never collided."

The thought stirs even more unexpected emotion, a reminder that none of this might have ever happened if I checked a different board or if Sunny somehow managed to make it to my gate.

Brett must read the hesitation still plastered on my face. He steps in so we're toe-to-toe, then presses a soft kiss to the side of my head. "You can do it, Nell," he encourages, his voice soft but serious.

My eyes fall shut slowly as I inhale deeply. "Pre-adventure?" I clarify, using all the confidence I can muster.

He winks, and goosebumps trail up my arm, making me forget what I was ever worried about—momentarily. "Pre-adventure."

The idea is ridiculous—me sitting here sketching him, pretending I don't know why he's dreading going home or the way he looks coming undone. Like I don't know *him* even after such a short time together. Not to mention that I don't do this. I don't just draw in front of people, not anymore, and especially in a crowded airport full of strangers.

But silly—and terrifying—as it seems, something about Brett and his deep dimples makes me want to oblige. Call it the effects of the day or the Christmas spirit or the lingering high I've been riding since, well... riding him—but my instinct is to do it. To go against my natural urge to shut down and draw him as if we never met. As if we never had our airport adventure. As if he was still a stranger.

"I'll do it," I blurt before I get a chance to chicken out.

His reaction is everything, and it's all the confidence I need. "Alright, you were standing here," he says, jumping right in and pointing to the ground beneath my feet. "And I was sitting there." He gestures to a spot where a woman is nursing her baby, then whips back around. Grinning awkwardly, he points to an empty chair a few seats from her. "But there's close enough."

I giggle, following him as he walks to the chair and sits, setting his backpack on the floor against his ankles. "Now draw me, Nellie Joy," he calls across the room. I shush him, glancing around to find most people either unaware or uninterested that Brett and I are having ourselves a less naked, role-reversed, Titanic moment.

When I bring my attention back to him, Brett is sitting back in his seat, his arm tossed over the chair beside him. He's watching me watch him, his eyes full of playfulness and intensity—just like he is. I unzip my backpack, reaching down to grab my sketchbook without breaking eye contact. When I find it, I pull my pencil from the front pocket and sit down on the floor underneath the board.

Finally tearing my eyes off of him, I flip open the book to a crisp white page. Brushing my palm down the heavyweight paper, the usual tightness that grows in my chest starts to build. The sadness that follows begins showing its face, lumping in my throat and weighing down my wrist.

It's not a sorrow that comes because I haven't made it—because I haven't found a path where my art is at the center. Instead, it's a grief over what I've lost—the joy and excitement of doing what I love. Rejection is hard. And like Brett said, I try to find the good in it. But how do you accept that what you thought your life would be just... isn't?

I stare at the page—the blank canvas waiting for me—and just like I did in the Uber here, I push past the pain and put my pencil to paper. When I peer up at Brett, he's still looking at me, his smile wide and eyes innocent, and my breath comes just a little easier.

I drag my hand across the paper, the first stroke lighter than I expected. I trace over it, my sketchbook balanced on one knee, capturing the angle of Brett's body as I look upward at it. Instead of skewing my perception,

I decide to draw him exactly how I see him, gravity pulling everything down, shadows spilling over the arms of the chair.

Time passes—I'm not sure how long—but eventually, his body takes shape on the page. I bring my gaze up to meet his smile as I build the rough outline of his face and realize the tightness from before has completely dissolved. I hide my grin, dropping my attention to his chin, too invested to allow myself to be distracted by his puppy dog eyes.

I shape the slope of his cheekbones, the slight scrunch in his nose from the arch in his lips, and then shade my favorite dimples. I draw his hair, the layers of light and dark creating texture, one rebellious lock falling onto his forehead. Then come the finishing touches—a laugh line here, a shadow there, those long lashes that frame his beautiful round eyes.

I scan the final product, giggling as I consider adding the bucket hat on his head from memory. Brett stifles a chuckle himself, completely unaware of what set me off. It hits me that I've ended up exactly where he wanted me to be—having fun again with a pencil in my hand.

I don't know if it's him, the craziness of the whole situation or if it really did stir something deep inside me. But as I look at the piece, I don't second guess whether it's good enough. For once, I'm not worried about purpose or perfection. Instead, I find joy in getting lost in a moment. In creating something. In capturing a memory.

"I guess I didn't account for the fact that you were looking up from the ground." Brett's words pull me from my trance as I whip my head over my shoulder, not even noticing he moved until now. "Not my best angle," he laughs.

"No," I throw back. "I think it's perfect." I smudge a harsh line on the hand around his cup. "You look celestial, powerful—larger than life."

My voice comes out soft—reflective—almost as taken aback as I am by everything that just transpired.

"I barely know what that means," Brett whispers playfully in my ear.

His warm breath floats past my neck, and I find myself leaning toward him. "Like the sun," I say.

Brett looks almost through me as his smile fades and his eyes turn eager. He reaches for my arm, his palm sliding down my sleeve. When his hand reaches mine, he links only our pinky fingers together. "Nellie, I—"

"Attention all Golden City travelers..." A voice spews from the speakers, pushing us apart. "All flights have now been rescheduled, and all departure boards have been updated. Please make sure to check your trip details for the latest information. Thank you for your patience. From all of us here at Golden City Airport, we wish you a very Merry Christmas Eve!"

Brett sighs as the announcement fades, his eyes slowly falling shut. "I guess it's time to go."

12

Brett

"**S**o, which one are you?"

I scan the board, looking for any other places where I might find my destination listed next to a different time. When I'm unsuccessful, I blow a breath through my lips, my stomach dropping with my chest. "First one," I say, pointing to the top of the list. "Flight 1225."

Nellie inhales sharply. "Oh," she says in a tone that sounds more painful than I'm sure she intended. "I guess you'll be out of here before you know it then." She forces a faint smile, tightening the grip on the handle of her carry-on.

"About an hour," I say, admitting out loud what I wish wasn't true.

Nellie swallows hard, avoiding my gaze. "Well, then... I win. I'll be here the longest."

I inhale slowly, tightening the grip on the straps of my backpack. "Feels like a lose-lose to me, honestly." Her head snaps in my direction. "You know, because it means we're either stuck here longer or forced to face reality?" She searches my eyes, attempting to determine my honesty—or motive. "Right?" I press.

"Uh, yeah, right." She licks her lips, and I physically falter. "Home or... stuck."

I suck my teeth and nod. "Unless..." Her eyes widen as she hangs on to my every word. "Unless that wouldn't be so horrible?"

"Going home?" she asks quickly.

I arch a brow and shrug. "Or staying here."

She blinks rapidly, like she's unsure of whether to agree—or fully show her cards. "Yeah, no. Neither would be... terrible." Her voice trails off as the board refreshes and *Now Boarding* flashes next to my flight number.

"Shit," I whisper under my breath.

"I guess now we'll never know." She smiles up at me unconvincingly and pulls her carry-on closer to her.

In *my* head, it's as if we're caught in this dance—a back and forth where neither of us wants to be the first to admit we might actually feel something. My gut swears she feels the same pit in her stomach about our time finally coming to an end. But how can I be sure? Like before, I wonder if Nellie and I really are an exception, or if I'm just seeing what I *want* to see... again.

My thoughts flip-flop between my feelings and Helen's voice until the flashing green words on the departure board remind me that I have a plane to catch. Right then, I decide I don't care how it looks. If this is the last time I see her, I'm not leaving with anything left unfinished.

"Nellie, listen—"

"Burnsey?" A squeaky voice cuts me off, followed by a tiny hand tugging on my arm.

I glance down to see a boy, maybe eight, beaming up at me while his parents watch in the background as if Christmas came early.

My eyes flick to Nellie, who's staring at me again. I'm tempted to ask the kid to give me just one second, but between his mile-wide smile and my heartstrings, there's no way I could. "Hey, buddy," I say, crouching down. "How's it goin'?"

His face somehow grows brighter as he whips out a pen and one of those useless brown paper towels. "Can you sign this?" he asks eagerly. "It's all I could find."

I get lost in the memory of being pressed next to Nellie on that supply closet floor, our lips almost touching, then clear my throat. "Oh, uh..."

I slide my backpack from my shoulder, unzipping the biggest pocket, searching for something else to give him.

"Here." Nellie appears beside me, flipping her sketchbook to a clean white page. "This is better." She winks at the little boy, and we both light up.

"Thanks, lady!"

I put my bag back on and take the book from Nellie, trying to tell her with only eye contact what I was about to say before this, then force my gaze away. I grab the pen from the boy and grin. "Turn around."

He does, and I unnecessarily lean the pad on his back. His parents shoot him a thumbs up in the background as I ask him his name.

"Leo," he says.

"Woah..." I press the pen to paper and write out the letters. "Brave like a lion, huh?"

"On and off the ice!" he chirps.

I laugh, finishing my signature and tearing out the page. "You know, Leo, Nellie here says *I'm* like a puppy. What do you think?"

He squints, studying me, then nods. "I can see it."

I chuckle, handing him the autograph. "Yeah." I glance at her. "Me too." Nellie's smile softens, and I turn back to Leo.

"Thank you!" he says, his eyes glued to the paper.

"You got it, bud." I hold out my fist, and he knocks his into it before running toward his family. "I'll see you at a game one day, maybe."

"Okay!" he calls over his shoulder. I wave at his parents, then shove my hands into my pockets.

"You should go," Nellie says before I can even face her.

I open my mouth—ready to argue, say anything—but nothing comes out.

"Go, Brett," she repeats gently. Those two words knock the wind out of me, but her expression tells me she doesn't mean them harshly. "You can't miss this flight. Not after all this. Your family's waiting for you—they've waited long enough. And you guys have a conversation to get to. One you're ready for."

I stand there, her words—and my thoughts—colliding with the message on the board overhead. My mind races as I try to recover from this quick back and forth. Maybe I did blow this up in my mind. Maybe the thought of landing in uncertainty back home made me cling to the only steady thing here.

Still thrown, I nod slowly. "Uh, yeah." I shake my head trying to ground myself. "Yeah, okay."

"This has been fun," she says. She hesitates, then pushes through, slipping her hand into mine. "Thank you, Brett. For everything."

I swallow the lump in my throat, my words stuck behind it. I want to thank her too—for passing the time, for the adventure. For all of it. But the truth is, if I even open my mouth, every declaration and confession I was ready to admit will pour out with it.

So, instead, I pull her close. I wrap my arms around her neck, nuzzling my face into the cinnamon-scented red hair that drew me to her in the first place. Nellie clings to me, her arms around my waist, and we stay like that until she finally pulls away.

"Go," she whispers.

I press my lips together, fighting every instinct not to, then I lean down and kiss her forehead. "I'll see ya, Angel."

With that, I turn and walk away without looking back. Because I can't. Because if I do, I won't leave at all.

My steps feel heavy, the crowd around me blurring as I head toward my gate, almost as if I'm walking through water. My mind flashes through our time together like a movie montage, and I get lost in the film, pressing forward despite feeling like I'm moving against the current.

I walk for I'm not sure how long, trying to distract myself by thinking of everything I'm flying into.

My family.

My secret.

Countless traditions.

One conversation.

But nothing works.

Suddenly, there's a hand on my shoulder, and I freeze.

Every nerve tingles, and every hair on my body stands on end. My eyes sink shut as I suck in a breath, hoping—praying—this means she felt it too.

I spin around slowly, preparing and torturing myself all at once.

"I think you dropped this."

A flight attendant in uniform holds out a bold yellow wad of fabric. I stare at it, her arm still outstretched patiently, then force myself to reach back and take it. "Thank you," I manage. The woman smiles politely then strides down the hallway, leaving me standing there alone, bucket hat in hand.

I reach for my backpack, hanging open, and realize I must have never zipped it back up as I was looking for something to autograph for Leo. I slap the hat back inside, adding it to the rest of its contents, and closing it up as if it's just another worn t-shirt or faded pair of jeans that I packed for home.

The souvenir is so simple—so ridiculous, really—but I somehow feel better knowing it's with me. I face the direction of my gate again, but as I take the next weighty step, it hits me. *That's* exactly how I feel about this adventure with Nellie.

It was uncomplicated—effortless. We were both stuck here, so we spent time together. But it was also a little crazy. The secrets we told, the things we did... they don't make sense for two perfect strangers. Yet somehow, I felt better just knowing she was there.

The problem is now I don't.

She's gone, and I have no way to reach her, and despite everything we talked about, so much has been left unsaid. I glance down at my watch, knowing that I'm risking everything I've waited for, but before I can stop myself... I turn back around.

I rush back, bobbing and weaving around people as if I'm on ice, gliding so quickly my shoes become skates. Adrenaline courses through me as I look for her like a lifeline, the very real possibility I miss the flight I've waited over twelve hours for looming in my mind.

Sooner than I expect, she comes into view—her striking red hair glowing like the light at the end of a tunnel. At first, I think my eyes are playing tricks on me, like when you're in park and a car drives past you, making it seem like you're rolling backward. There's no way I'm moving this fast.

But when I get closer, I see that's not it at all. Her sleeves—those damn angel wings—are trailing behind her. I'm not running that quickly. It only feels that way because she's running too.

Meeting me halfway.

"What are you doing?" she pants when I finally reach her.

"What are *you* doing?" I ask, my breath also heavy.

Nellie reaches behind her and slides a rolled up paper from her back pocket. "I was bringing you this." She hands it to me as my mind runs a mile a minute. "Aren't you going to miss your flight?"

I look down at the tube in my hand. "No," I answer, sliding it open. "No, I'll be..."

My voice fades as realization sets in.

"Fine," I finish, unveiling the rest of her sketch.

"I thought you might want to keep it, ya know? As a reminder of... whatever."

My eyes lift to hers. "A souvenir?"

She shrugs, smiling shyly. "I know it's not a bucket hat, but—"

My lips cut her off as they slam into hers, my one hand on the best gift I could ask for.

The other on the drawing.

Nellie sinks into me, her hands flying to the hem of my sweater as she scrunches it in her white-knuckled grip. I slide my palm past her cheek, and she wraps her arms around my waist.

The crowd around us keeps moving—like a scene from a movie where the camera circles the couple kissing in an otherwise uninterrupted hallway. People flow past us, some stopping to gawk, I'm sure, but in the small space where Nellie and I are intertwined, the world stands still.

Here, in this moment, everything changes. Much like earlier when I knew being with her would separate the rest of my experiences into *befores* and *afters,* I know with everything in me that this moment will count. Like a last minute penalty when you're already down or an empty net goal when you're up by one, this instant—this kiss—will seal our fate.

"Brett, you have to go," Nellie reminds me, breaking our embrace. Her palm lands on my chest, and I swear she hits my heart.

"Not before you tell me what happens next. With us." I brush my thumb over her bottom lip, wiping away the rest of our kiss.

"Brett..."

"No," I stop her. "I'm not leaving again without asking."

"Brett, I just—"

"Nellie, this was more than wasting time, wasn't it?" I take her hand in mine and pull it close. "It had to be. I mean, the laughs and the secrets... the Sleep Suite? There has to be more than this, right?"

She peers up and gives my hand a tight squeeze. "It was way more than wasting time." My lungs inflate as I smile wide. Nellie closes what little gap is left between us, grabbing my other hand and bringing both between us. "It was an adventure."

My face starts to fall as her words—and her tone—sink in. "There's a *but* coming, isn't there?"

She hangs her head between her arms. When she looks up at me, her eyes are glossy. "But... maybe we should leave it at that. Let this be what it was—two strangers who helped each other through more than just the passing of time."

I part my lips to argue—to throw back that we aren't strangers. Not at all. But the reality is, she's right. We don't know each other outside of these walls or circumstances. I don't know what she's like on Monday mornings or if she loads forks in the dishwasher prongs up or down. All I know is that I'm leaving this place better than I got here. Happier, more confident.

Changed because of her.

Nellie knows pieces of me, that much is true. Pieces that, honestly, only she holds. And maybe she's right. Maybe this entire experience—this whole adventure—would be best left as exactly that. A memory. A blip in our lives where we bared our souls on a supply closet floor and relied on each other to stay sane in an overcrowded airport at Christmas.

Or maybe not.

"Nah," I answer, dropping her hands and shaking my head. "I'm not into that."

She tilts her chin down and smirks before her whole body deflates. "I just..."

"What?" I ask, sliding my palm past her cheek. "Say it."

She lets out a deep breath and peers up at the ceiling. "I just don't want to ruin this, ya know? Right now it feels magical because, well... it is. But when we're back in the real world..." Her words fade out, but I know what she's saying.

"We'll be out of our bubble."

She nods sweetly. "Our snow globe."

I take a deep breath, readying myself for the words that are about to pour from my mouth. "What if we let fate decide?"

Her forehead creases as she waits for me to continue.

"What if we don't exchange numbers or look each other up? What if we just see if our paths cross again?"

Nellie settles her weight on one hip and tucks both hands into her back pockets. "Brett..." she says, her name slicing through my chest the same way it always does. "Do you really think that's possible? I mean, what are the chances we find each other twice in this massive city?"

I smile coyly, running my tongue across my teeth. "I'm gonna guess... less than one percent."

She smiles, her green eyes twinkling back at me. "You know, I've heard that happens more than you'd think."

I nod, soaking up every second of studying her just like this. "I like my odds."

"It's settled then." She links her pinky with mine and gives it a squeeze.

I step toe-to-toe with her, leaning down and pressing my forehead against hers. I breathe in her cinnamon scent and the refreshing feeling of this—of her and of me—being just enough.

"Merry Christmas, Brett," Nellie says, her evergreen eyes hopeful on me.

I kiss her gently, then stand back, just in time to see the sun rising through the windows. The snow has stopped, but flurries float off of the mounds piled high on the building. They swirl around the tarmac, sparkling in the light.

I look back at Nellie, glowing from the beams that stream through the glass, and smile.

Still an angel.

"Merry Christmas, Nellie."

Epilogue - Nellie
Ten Weeks Later

I've never been one to draw buildings. Something about the harsh lines and rigidity have always been threatening. Unlike people or plants or the side profile of potential serial killers, there's no room for mistakes when you're dealing with architecture. Things would look ridiculous if even one angle was off.

I attempted to sketch Frostpine Fall's Town Hall the last time I was home, and it came out looking like a wax version of a sad Barbie Dreamhouse. I guess it's just not in my nature to be so technical with my work—and my hands aren't steady enough to make straight lines freely.

But that's why I've been practicing.

There's a brownstone right outside of Drippy's, with overflowing flower pots at the top of the steps, and a bright red door that stands out against the classic copper exterior. It's been the perfect subject. The buds on the stairs have been blooming, the sweetest reminder that spring is finally here, and that beautiful Flames-colored door always brings me back to... *him*.

I haven't seen Brett since our airport adventure. In reality, I could go to a game and somehow make myself known or slide into one of his many DMs. But we made a promise to each other that only fate would decide if we were meant to meet again. And although I'm not waiting for him,

I'm also not willing to settle for anything but our less than one percent chance.

"Can I take this from you?"

I glance up to see the teenage busboy who floats around Drippy's, gesturing to my now empty mug. "Oh, sure," I say, dragging my eyes away from the apartment across the street. "Thank you."

The kid takes the cup and shuffles away, the hem of his overly baggy pants dragging on the floor. I pick up my pencil and refocus myself on the shadow the railing of the brownstone casts on the sidewalk. Before I can shade underneath the dark line, my stomach growls loud enough that I'm afraid pedestrians heard it outside.

I inhale deeply, arching away the ache in my back. The stiffness in my shoulders tells me I've been hunched over this counter by the window for entirely too long without a break or sustenance. "Not again," I groan, unsure of how many times this past month I've sat and drawn for hours on end fueled by caffeine and stubbornness alone.

Standing from my stool, I set my pencil down and grab my purse and phone from beside my sketchbook. I'm not ready to give up yet—those bay windows live rent-free in my mind—but the edges and angles are hard enough without the blur of hunger playing a factor.

I move toward the line that's just a few customers deep, reading a text from my mom about her visit next weekend. I get to the back just as those waiting move up and try to look over the shoulder of the massively broad person in front of me to see if there happen to be any more French vanilla muffins left in the display case. When it's apparent that I won't be able to see the pastries until the giant in joggers with his hood over his head is out of my way, I take out my phone. I pull up Instagram and begin to scroll, dodging spoilers from last night's *Love Island* episode.

"Hello?" a voice rings out from in front of me. I assume it belongs to the guy whose sole purpose before this was to block my view of the muffin case, but I can't be sure. I'm only half paying attention to the world around me because the other half of my focus is playing a game of chicken with the possibility that I learn who's been dumped from the island thanks to pop-up photos from Casa Amor.

"Okay, yeah, I'll be there in ten. I'm just grabbing coffee. Yes, I got you one. Yep. Alright, I'll see ya soon."

Swiping open my texts, I hear his words faintly as I respond to my mom's last message. I type out that no, she doesn't need to pay ahead for a bus ticket, and yes, we can eat at one of those taco trucks she's seen on the Food Network that parks on the streets. Then, just as I hit send, the guy steps up to the counter.

"Two black coffees, please," he says simply.

It's only four words—one pretty standard order—but for some reason, it captures my full attention. There's something about the way they're said, the cadence maybe, or the accent attached. But I'm pulled a step closer, my toes nearly at his heels as I wait for him to speak again.

Only moments later, the barista walks from the coffee machine back to the counter. I lose her behind his figure, but I hear the tear of a receipt and a familiar *thank you* that takes my breath away. Before it fully registers—before I can fully wrap my mind around what's happening—the person in front of me turns to leave, and I forget exactly how close behind him I am.

"Oh my God."

"Oh, shit."

There's a fumble between us—of words and apologies and two steaming hot coffees. Luckily, in the time that's passed, his grasp on a to-go cup seems to have improved.

Him.

"Woah, I'm so... sorry." Brett's voice fades out as his gaze moves from the drinks in his hands up to me. "Nellie."

"Hey." I stand in awe of him—of *this*—only capable of getting one word out as I meet the same puppy dog eyes from almost three months ago.

"Hi," he says back, just as simply.

We stand like that, taking each other in, until an elderly woman behind me clears her throat. Brett nods toward an empty space at the end of the counter, and I follow him like no time has passed at all.

"What are you..." He sets the cups down and reaches for his hood, pulling it down and showing off that beautiful head of hair. "How have you been?"

I take a deep breath, my eyes wide, my mind searching for the answer like it's someone else's life. "Good," I respond. "Great, actually. I, um... I'm here... drawing." I tip my chin toward the spot at the window where my sketchbook still sits waiting for me.

"Wow," he says breathlessly. He smiles, and the dimples that visit me in my dreams finally show their face in real life. "That's... that's awesome. I'm so glad you're back at it."

I nod, licking my lips, and Brett's gaze drops to them briefly. "Uh, yeah," I stutter, dragging my eyes away from him. I stare just past him, regulating myself enough to say the next part out loud. "I actually draw quite a bit now. I got a job a few weeks ago working in art therapy for kids."

Brett's breath hitches as his mouth falls open. He drags his palm down his face as he settles his hip against the counter. "That's perfect," he says softly. I smile up at him, and he cracks his neck to one side, gathering himself and standing straight again. "Big fan of therapy," he adds, pointing to his chest.

I choose my next words wisely—how creepy am I willing to sound? But all things considered, I decide I don't care. If there was ever a time that called for full-disclosure, it's this one. "You actually gave me the idea," I admit.

His eyebrows shoot up as he shoves his hands into the pockets of his joggers.

"The way you just took the pressure off for me—I mean, drawing you in the airport was just about the most cathartic experience I think I've ever had. Then, just talking with you about therapy... I don't know, it just came to me. On the plane ride home, actually."

"That's awesome, Nell. Helen would be proud." I laugh shyly and look down at my hands. "Wait," he says. My eyes dart back to him. "Does that mean you aren't working with Ruthie anymore?"

I shake my head with enthusiasm. "No, actually. I mean, I'm not working directly for Liam as her nanny, but she comes to see me for art therapy each week. Liam was great about the whole thing, of course—encouraged it, even. I looked for jobs while he looked for my replacement, and I still see them both, which works out for everyone."

"I'm so happy for you," he says, his eye contact as intense as it's ever been, his expression full of pride.

"How'd things go with your family?" I ask, flipping the attention. "And your dad?"

Brett sighs heavily, but not with discontent. With relief. "Great, actually," he answers, stealing my words. "My mom doesn't necessarily want to be a part of the reunion, but she was completely supportive of me doing what I have to do. Tom and Bailey said the same. My sister actually came with me the first time I met up with him. She hung back, but she dropped me off and waited just in case I needed an out."

I smother my natural instinct, which is to tell him how amazing she sounds, and how much I'd love to meet her. "Sounds like she really is a grown up now, huh?" I say instead.

"It's terrifying," he laughs.

I chuckle too. "I get that."

"But my dad's been... around. That's who this other one's for." He points to one coffee with drops along the rim from our near collision. He takes a napkin from the holder beside them and wipes at them as he continues. "We've been meeting pretty regularly. His new job has him coming here a few times each month, so it's been easier to get to know him." He exhales, then looks right at me. "It finally feels like everything's falling into place again."

A silence settles between us, one loaded with questions and the passing of time. I don't rush to fill it. I've thought about this moment for weeks, and now that it's here, I just want to savor it.

I don't know if he's found someone else in the meantime. I don't know if, outside of our snow globe, he looks back and laughs at how ridiculous we were. Does he even still think about me the way I still think about him? Or does he regret the holiday delay we spent together at Christmas?

"Oh," Brett says out of nowhere.

He reaches for his wallet and opens up the money slot. Reaching past the bills that sit inside, he digs with his thumb and forefinger to the bottom of the leather. When he finds what he's looking for, he holds it up, the silver catching in the light.

"I got this for you from Barksdale. I thought if I ever saw you again you might want to add it to your plane, if you still have it. It's a tree, you know, because of the..." Brett reads my blank face as something other than the shock and overwhelming joy I feel. "Name," he finishes, shaking his head and lowering the charm. "It's stupid, really."

"It's not stupid." I intercept it as he tries to return it to the slot, pulling it from his fingers and cherishing it in mine.

Brett smiles wide, then swallows hard, putting his wallet back into his pocket. "If it were a dog, it might be cooler."

I nod, and his face falls slightly. "A puppy maybe." It lights up again. "I love it, thank you."

I lift my left wrist and show off my bracelet with one lone charm dangling from the bottom. The one I've worn every day since my flight landed that day. I attempt to clip the tree next to it, but the metal on the chain shifts each time I do.

"Here, let me."

Brett reaches for me, his fingers warm as they graze my wrist. He holds the bracelet in one hand and the charm in the other, effortlessly hooking it around a single link. Our faces are close, him leaning down, still gripping my arm. That same sweet, musky smell from before floats off of him, and just like that, I'm right back in the airport.

"Hey."

My eyes spring to his, every fiber of my being on edge for what's next.

Brett leans back against the counter. "Would you maybe want to get together sometime? You know... eat a meal that doesn't come from a machine or sit at an actual table for a drink?" He gives me that boyish grin, and everything around us melts away. "No carolers, I promise."

I nearly snort as I remember the French rendition of *Blue Christmas*, but somehow hold it together to answer. "Yeah," I say. *We beat the odds after all.* "I'm free right now, actually. If..."

"Oh, I, uh..." He looks back at the two cups still sitting on the counter.

"You're meeting your dad," I say, shaking my head, trying to hide my disappointment. "Duh. You just said that."

"I am," he confirms, and my stomach sinks. "But he only has like an hour. I can swing back this way and pick you up after?"

My entire mood lifts, and I don't even attempt to conceal it. "Okay."

"Yeah?"

I nod, and both of us smile. A weight I didn't know I was carrying lifts slowly from my shoulders.

"Cool," he says, his expression full of excitement. "Should I text you when I'm on my way?"

The question's so casual. Of course he should, that's what people do. But the idea of having direct access to each other feels foreign. Foreign and so damn exhilarating. We no longer have to wait for *chance* to decide that we should see each other. That we were meant to meet.

Because it already did.

"Sure."

He hands me his phone, and I type in my number. I give it back to him, and he taps on the screen to save it.

"Okay," he says, reaching for the cups. He stands there, his hands full, and I'm glad.

Because it's the only reason I don't throw my body into his.

"Okay," I repeat, my lips curling upward.

Brett gives me a knowing look, then walks past me. I follow him, smiling when he looks back before pushing through the door.

Once he's out of sight, I sink onto a stool at the corner of the counter, drained in the best way from our interaction. And from knowing the wait is finally over.

I glance over at my sketchbook, already having forgotten about the French vanilla muffin that may or may not be sitting in the case, but before I can move to it, my phone buzzes twice. I look down, expecting to see Mom questioning the best place to take a picture of the Golden City skyline or whether she should say hi when she walks past someone on the street.

But it's not.

Instead, it's two texts, one right after another.

Both from an unknown number—a stranger.

Yet... not at all.

Unknown Number

Still an angel.

Unknown Number

I'll see you soon.

The End

Acknowledgements

To those who begged to see more of Brett "Burnsey" Burns—thank you. It's because of you that this Golden Retriever finally found his girl.

With lots of love (& tons of angst—the good kind, obviously),
Cassandra

About The Author

Cassandra Moll is a hockey wife and girl mom to three little ladies who are the inspiration behind her imprint name - *Three Bows Books*. When she's not chasing them around, Cassandra loves to be outside, lift weights, and read. After falling back in love with books, and hearing other authors' stories, she was inspired to finally write her own. Cassandra's books are filled with love and angst and sprinkled with banter that keeps you coming back for more.

For more information about Cassandra and her books, please visit cassandramoll.com.